I hid behind a gravestone and watched Angie Hutchinson go down to where my daffodil heart lay blooming by Mr Tyson's grave. Angie knelt on the grass and closely inspected the flowers growing there. She looked right inside the trumpet parts and fondled the petals. Finally, with a quick pull, she yanked out one of those Mystics. Hiding it under her jacket, she stalked off the way she'd come.

Angie Hutch had in her possession, clutched close to her breathing body, a daffodil that I had planted! It was almost like she was pressing me to her heart.

I'd love anyone for ever who could help me out of this mess . . . I'd love them with a passion.

That was what she'd said earlier. And it was me, Andrew Kindness, who held the key to Angie's happiness. All I had to do was come clean about my private passion for daffodils, help her make a triumph of this BBC thing, and be swept into sweet bliss for ever. Those were her own words. *For ever.* She'd promised it.

www.rbooks.co.uk

Also by Gareth Thompson

THE GREAT HARLEQUIN GRIM

SUNSHINE *to the* SUNLESS

GARETH THOMPSON

DEFINITIONS

SUNSHINE TO THE SUNLESS
A DEFINITIONS BOOK 978 1 862 30467 3

First published in Great Britain by Definitions,
an imprint of Random House Children's Books
A Random House Group Company

This edition published 2008

1 3 5 7 9 10 8 6 4 2

The Random House Group Limited makes every effort to ensure that
the papers used in its books are made from trees that have been legally
sourced from well-managed and credibly certified forests. Our paper
procurement policy can be found at: www.randomhouse.co.uk/paper.htm

Mixed Sources
Product group from well-managed
forests and other controlled sources
www.fsc.org Cert no. TT-COC-2139
© 1996 Forest Stewardship Council
FSC

Definitions are published by Random House Children's Books,
61–63 Uxbridge Road, London W5 5SA

www.**kids**at**randomhouse**.co.uk
www.rbooks.co.uk

Addresses for companies within The Random House Group Limited can be found at:
www.randomhouse.co.uk/offices.htm

THE RANDOM HOUSE GROUP Limited Reg. No. 954009

A CIP catalogue record for this book is available from the British Library.

Printed in the UK by CPI Bookmarque, Croydon, CR0 4TD

From one AGT to another

ONE

At the sweet age of nine I saw my coastline commit double murder. There was no other human witness to the final killing. Only the circling seabirds that cried like stray kittens.

I can look down on myself as the gulls would have seen me. A stodgy little boy wearing a woolly hat and cheap red tracksuit. A cloudy Sunday in mid-March. I was alone on the shores of Millom's estuary.

The small town lies on the south-west coast of Cumbria, in the forgotten zone of the Lake District. The bay is an outlet for the river Duddon, whose waters get broken up by old marshland, then trickle through. At high tide the bay fills from the Irish Sea, away to the west.

The estuary is only a mile wide at some points. That's why people think they can walk safely over it. Across the bay from Millom lies the Barrow peninsula, where shady shipyards build nuclear submarines. You can see cranes and tall towers against a backdrop of mountains.

The bay is full of sandy channels like a ploughed field. As water runs into these furrows, it causes tiny whirlpools. But some of the channels are three metres wide. You can't leap from one side to another. Crabs and crayfish scuttle across them at low tide.

It was cold and dreary by four o'clock. I had been bird-watching in the wooden observation hut that over-looks Millom's blue lagoons. This hut stands just beyond the beach near an old lighthouse, where the bay curves around. The lagoons lie inland as you walk towards town. Deep below them are Millom's old iron-mining works, now sunken like Atlantis.

After leaving the bird-watching hut I went eastwards around the big bulge of bay. The land there was all shingle or grassy scrub. At last I felt wet sand under my feet. The tide was drifting in. I watched a little tern stab its long yellow beak into the damp beach. Its pointed white wings were huge and feathery. They rose up from the tern's back like an angel's. And above me a peregrine falcon flew towards the lagoon, drawn by the swarms of birds there. It wore a hunter-killer's dark brown cloak.

Staring over the bleak bay, I saw a dash of colour through the mist. Somebody was making the dangerous walk across the sands from Askam.

I tried to focus with watery eyes. Then the weather cleared and brightened for a minute. It was long enough for me to make out two people, and hear one voice. A man's voice, angry and frustrated. The sound carried eerily.

'Can you not understand?' the man shouted. 'Must I always do everything for you?'

A boy, wearing a beaming T-shirt, pulled away from the man. Hands thrust in jeans pockets, he stumbled over sandy ridges.

The man yelled out again, 'I asked you to do something quite simple. Did I not?'

The boy mooched away even further. He kicked out at the ground, creating a sudden splash. The man stopped, hands on hips, and tipped his head to the heavens. I gripped my bird-watching binoculars, wanting to zoom in on this private drama.

I looked through the glasses, twisting the focus dial until I had a clear picture ahead. By now the two figures were a hundred metres away. They knocked around towards me, the boy drifting further to the man's right. He walked all hunched up, as if sulking. He kicked the wet and rutted sand again. But this time his foot stayed stuck. He fell forward like some animal caught in a trap.

The man didn't glance across. Face towards me, he seemed to catch sight of this distant onlooker in a red tracksuit. I looked away, ashamed of spying, and peered back at that boy in his bright shirt.

It was like he had turned to stone. He stood with legs apart, as if to let a pet dog pass through. Seagulls hovered on the breeze above, like spirits caught between heaven and earth. I wanted them to swoop down and carry the boy far away.

I tried to shout a warning. 'It's very soft out there! It's not like solid ground that supports your weight!' In the end I only whispered it, my throat already drying.

The man looked over at the struggling lad, who was trying to haul each leg out in turn. Then the boy's first cry, 'I'm stuck,' rang out with a hint of panic.

'Honest, Dad, I'm stuck.'

The sky was dour. Mist was creeping down dark hills on the far shore, ready to settle over Askam for the evening. For a moment I left the two humans and viewed the background mountains. Their colours were a quilt of green bracken, purple heather, yellow gorse and black rock. But they sat there like stony judges, unwilling to alter any human fate.

I switched back to that man and boy in the bay. And suddenly my grip grew even hotter on the field glasses.

TWO

The boy's face was visible now. It was a sickly white colour. He looked a right weakling, with stick-like limbs. His father was on his knees, a little bald man with brainy round specs. He was furiously trying to dig out his son with bare hands. But the more he dug, the more everything oozed back around him. It was a sandy slop, yet the boy was held in its vice-like grip.

The father looked up and caught sight again of my red shape.

'Come here!' he shouted. 'Quick! We need help!'

I could hear my own harsh breathing, like the north wind at your door. Blood throbbed in my ears, so that all other noise was reduced. The gulls wheeling above, looking for fishy scraps, were cut to a dim screech.

Before the mist came down again, I saw the detail on that boy's shirt. By now he was up to his knees in quicksand. His top was yellow, with an orange circle on the front. It was like watching a daffodil drowning in mud.

The man was fumbling with a mobile phone. In his haste he dropped it, and scrabbled around in soft silt. As he tried to stand he toppled back, but his own stuck feet held him fast. He was also caught now. Father and son began to go under in slow motion, as if the sands must savour every moment.

My throat was as dry as dark earth. 'Don't struggle,' I tried to scream. 'They always tell you not to struggle. Just stay still and shout really loud.'

Nobody had told these two. The father flapped with windmill arms. His feeble son sobbed and struggled. The more they wriggled, the quicker the sucking sand gained a hold. My hands were so glued to the binocs, so petrified into position, that no power could have released them. I watched the terrible show like some evil voyeur.

That's when the man bawled at me with shocking violence. I wobbled on the spot as if hit by a gale. I finally ran to raise the alarm. But nobody was in sight along the windblown estuary, and the nearest houses were away in the small town.

Instead, I ran back around the bay. Going over rough grassland, I stumbled and fell by a gorse bush. Two fat bees were among its yellow flowers. They scratched about wildly for pollen, with black insect legs. Their fur was orange, like specks of sunshine.

I got up and panted into the wooden shed that overlooked the lagoon. A tall figure sat with elbows on the bench, field glasses to his eyes, looking through the window holes. He had long white hair, all wavy like it was freshly washed. He wore large specs, and had big sandals on his hairy feet. I thought of him as a strange wizard.

My throat felt choked but I blurted out two words. *'Please! Help!'*

Without waiting, I chased back across rough grass to the shore. Several minutes had passed since I'd left the man and boy alone. By now the boy's father was thigh-deep in the sandy ooze. It was like watching someone trapped in cement.

The phone was inches from his purple face. His round specs had fallen into the watery bay. He was gibbering at the mobile, making one final plea for mercy. His head jerked around, trying to identify any landmarks for the rescuers to latch onto. Before him lay the old slagbanks of Millom's mining past, now levelled out into raised beaches. Far behind him stood the windpower windmills over Kirkby Moor's lavender ridges. They rose like white stakes on some sacred hill.

That wizard man turned up, unsure what the panic was. He carried a light metal walking stick. He screwed up his old eyes and shoved both hands under his chin.

'Oh, no!' he breathed. He turned wildly, shouting. 'Please someone . . . please . . . !'

I watched him hobble into the shallows. He took each step as if it might be his last. We both knew he could do nothing. We both knew he wasn't going to risk himself.

The struggling father reached out to his son. Grabbing a twiggy arm, he cried, 'They're sending a helicopter! Just hang on, Simon!'

But Simon had struggled so hard to get free that he

was waist-deep, and still sinking. The two figures swayed in a thick quicksand soup. The tide was now swashing in from the Irish Sea. Any chance of a rescue would have to come before the bay filled, and it filled rapidly. They call the tide around these parts 'the galloping horse' because you can't outrun it.

The man took off his brown jacket, which had a leather collar. He leaned over from the ribs and tugged off the boy's top. Even a few less grams of weight might count.

The field glasses were glued to my eyes, digging in with a force that left my face bruised. Because I could see the man's lips move, his shouted words carried clearly.

'Simon! Stand totally still. That's what they told me.'

I jagged the binocs to the left. The boy screamed back, with a shrill madness.

'I can't stop it! It's pulling me under!'

He squirmed again. The father flung out a hand and held his boy's wrist. His arm went stiff with the effort, but he had no muscles, and his child sank suddenly as if a hole had opened below. The same hidden hollow quickly took the man deeper, until both of them were just neck and shoulders above.

By now the old wizard was wading back, with heavy splashes. He turned and shouted something hopeful to the stranded pair. Then he stretched out helpless hands towards me, his metal stick pointing, and limped off in Millom's direction.

Out on the bay, the father turned his burning face to Simon. Whatever he said, his son nodded and stared through flooding tears. His head shook with constant shudders. Maybe his father had made some vow of undying love. Both were too weak to fight any more. I'm sure their faces met mine over the grey distance. Even though I was only a smudged figure, they seemed so close I felt my nose could have rubbed theirs.

That's when wreaths of mist blew across, as if to deny me the final act. I remember rain stinging my face, and I swore that if those foggy vapours lifted, I would look away. I would lay down the binoculars and close my eyes.

But I didn't look away. As a brisk breeze came to clear the scene, I stood watching like someone obsessed. Through magnified eyes I picked out the final details. Man and boy lifted their chins and noses to the grey sky, straining for each breath. The bleak bay rolled over them. It only took one final quicksand suction.

They had been out walking and they ended up sinking.

I stayed rooted there, watching sea water flood the furrows and fill each one in turn. Anchored sailboats bobbed with sudden life. A seagull swooped and stabbed for fish. Sunshine broke through the cloud cover, turning distant Kirkby Moor to sweet lilac.

An age later, the tall grasses around me were stirred by wild currents. The rescue helicopter revolved above, scattering seabirds to the mountain horizon. It rattled and nose-dived, then took to the heights again. A giant yellow bird encased in metal. I viewed the helicopter in close-up, standing under its hurricane breaths.

Then I was plunging back to Mrs Tyson's class, last term in junior school. I remembered how she stood before us, tiny and tubby, with short grey hair. But her voice carried a dark warning in every word. She was scolding us about the dangers of playing alone on the estuary.

'The bay is not a playground, children! What is the bay not? What is it *not*?'

The yellow chopper was heading back up the channel, a blur of blades hacking the mist. Stones and sand and bushes were blitzed under its windstorm.

I whispered, as if my school teacher was right there before me. *'It is not a playground, Mrs Tyson. It is a death trap.'*

THREE

For myself, I reckon two things came out of that tragic day. The first was a crazy desire to feel solid ground under my feet. For ages after, I would run on tiptoes down pavements, or race across fields before they could open up below me. In my wild mind, every surface underfoot turned mushy and sucked me in. Concrete, clay, grass or grit – they were all the same. Each one appeared as a red-brown mulch, to the point where I didn't dare go further than our front doorstep.

The nightmares came thick and fast, always with me as the sinking victim. The daymares were just as bad. I would nod off in class at school, and wake up shrieking seconds later as the floor dissolved into wet sand. At least nobody laughed. I wore this gloomy air of doom, as the boy who once witnessed two tourists die. Or was it an air of shame? I was also the boy who was too slow to fetch help. I just watched them sink under.

The first answer was provided by my dad, on my tenth birthday. He bought me a skateboard. A sturdy orange one with big blue stars.

'There you go, Andy,' he said, handing over a package wrapped in newspaper. 'You need never fear the great outdoors again. Your feet will be safely above the ground at all times.'

I was hooked from the start. Even though the skateboard put only a short gap between me and the earth, it felt like a hundred miles of safety. I went everywhere on 'Orange Flyer', as I called it – even across the road to our neighbours', down the long mile to school, or into Millom for shopping. At last I had a solid platform to stand on, to travel on, that wouldn't suck me under.

'There he goes,' I'd hear people say. 'Skating away without a care in the world. He's the one who saw those two tourists drown on the sands. He only ran to fetch help when it was too late. Makes you wonder why . . .'

They'd never know why, because I'd never know why I froze that day. And I had more cares to carry than they'd ever bear. But at least I was back out in the real world.

I still avoided the estuary, as if some long-dead curse would waken if I troubled the place. That was the other thing to change. Before that fateful day I'd been a real beach boy, always coming home with shoes full of sand, or trousers salty with water. Now I needed a fresh focus, a new game, to keep me away from the shrubby shore.

That came from my Granddad Hebthwaite, when he still lived nearby. About a month after the two deaths, he took me down to the grassy scrub that overlooks the bay. On a patch of raised ground, strewn with old white rocks, we stopped. We were almost in line with where the tragedy happened. Granddad was a sturdy and kindly man, with black-rimmed glasses and silver hair. He was dressed in his best Sunday clothes, and held my hand tightly. I shrank against him in sight of the estuary, and begged to go home. I was still only nine at the time.

But Granddad stood firm. In a plastic bag he had a load of daffodil bulbs. In his back garden he'd been cross-breeding species of them for years. They turned out in all shades of orange, yellow, pink and white.

There was one called 'Golden Glory' that he wanted to plant in memory of the father and son I'd seen perish. Granddad chose a patch of earth, free from the ancient rubble all around. I knelt with my back to the bay as he got busy with a small spade and trowel. He dug and smiled, and said I was very brave to be there helping him. All the time I felt knives of blame being planted in my spine by the quicksand's ghosts.

'Are we nearly done, Granddad?' I kept asking.

'Nearly,' he answered, digging yet another hollow. His broad cheeks were red with sea winds and gardening. 'This last one goes right at the tip.'

I was too anxious to get away to ask what he was doing. It was only a year later, when I was ten, that Granddad took me down to see. He had to almost drag me through the narrow town streets and out into the wilds. I covered my eyes with shaking hands, back near the bay I'd avoided for a year. It was early April, a sunny spring day, and the coastline smelled of seaweed.

Granddad stopped beside me and gently prised my

hands away. There in front of us lay a perfect tree-shape, picked out with dark yellow daffodils. Three rows of daffodils stood in the shape of a tree's trunk. Then four lines of golden flowers came fanning out from the top. They lay there like yellow and green branches, pointing across the bay to the mountains beyond.

'The tree of life,' said Granddad. 'Or maybe it's the tree of knowledge. But it belongs to everyone now, and it will grow again every year. Right here. You'll see.'

It looked so beautiful, and I felt so purged of sin, that I began to cry.

'There, now,' said Granddad, pulling me close. 'There, now. These daffodils are called Golden Glories. They're a type I created myself.'

'They're beautiful, Granddad,' I sobbed. I stared in amazement at the flowery tree, laid out flat like it was freshly felled. No mighty oak would ever again look this grand. Then I asked, in a very small voice, 'Have they forgiven me? That man and his boy?'

'There's nothing to forgive,' said Granddad. 'Other people failed them that day. Not you.'

I rubbed my eyes with grubby fingers. Granddad knelt to inspect his flowers. He stroked the inside of some golden petals, inspecting the yellow dust on his fingertips.

I stared long and hard at the tree-shape of growing daffodils. It was like I'd finally found some kind of answer. However my granddad managed to conjure up such floral marvels, I wanted in on the secret. These bright flowers could fill my lonely hours and keep me clear of the estuary for ever. And maybe I had a chance to offer things of beauty to the world. A fair exchange for my cowardly actions a year before.

So that's how I came to start cross-breeding daffodils myself – only for me it was to be a very secret mission. Beautiful ideas don't always fit well into small towns, when you're young.

Four

Those two tourists I saw get smothered weren't the first to vanish here. Not by a long stretch. King James the First lost half his troops when they got bogged down in this bay.

In September 1917 a terrible gale blew across the Duddon estuary. A cargo vessel called the *Coniston*, carrying timber for Millom's iron mines, got into difficulty and sank. Shifting sands and tides in 1987 uncovered the rotting hull of the *Coniston*, with her wooden frame like the skeleton of a whale. The great mainsails and masts were all long gone, ripped away by time and tides.

In the nineteenth century, iron ore was discovered in Millom's gritty ground. So iron mining became the town's main industry, employing everyone except the shopkeepers, publicans and bookies. Boats came down the bay to collect iron during the world wars, taking it back across to Barrow for shipbuilding.

My Granddad Hebthwaite was one of the mining 'Red Men'. They got their name from the red dust that covered everything around the town. Granddad worked in the mines until the last pit was finally closed.

When the iron began to get used up inland, they looked at the cost of extending the mining out to sea. But then a giant haematite mountain was discovered in South Africa, and iron production kicked off there. Millom, and its workforce, became redundant.

Iron is still in the earth everywhere here. When it rains, the old roads that were once train tracks turn a rusty crimson. Back in its mining heyday, nobody in the town ever wore white. The iron dust would stain everything red.

Granddad Hebthwaite told me how they used to make the iron. First they would fire up the iron ore to a massive heat. Then all the impure stuff rose to the surface to be skimmed off. The hot metal was poured into ingot moulds to set.

Granddad always used to compare this process to life itself. He'd say, 'Skim off the scum, and you're sure to find a few good nuggets.'

I knew what he meant, but I always made him explain. I'd kneel beside him in the daffodil beds he tended in his back garden. He called his garden 'my little piece of heaven on earth'.

'Well, now,' he'd say. 'You'll come across folks in life who'll do you harm, or say bad things about you. But never forget how many gems there are too; how many fine friends are waiting somewhere. So, if you skim off the scum from this life, you'll find rich rewards just below.'

When we went out walking, we sometimes found iron nuggets in the scuffed old roads. Granddad used to pretend these were something else.

'Ah, that's very good,' he'd say, stooping to pick up what looked like prehistoric rock. 'A *gold* ingot, Andrew. Very valuable.'

Back at home I would lay this 'gold ingot' on my pillow, and hope I was forgiven for not acting quicker to save two lives. Some days I would kneel there and offer up a prayer too. And then I would feel more at peace.

Millom was covered with many other relics of its mining days. The streets in the old part of town were grid-like rows of terraced houses, where the miners used to live, back-to-back and side-by-side. Washing lines still hung across the yards, but some of the upper storeys had satellite dishes.

Across the town was a new estate, with posher houses, where people lived who worked at the shipyards in Barrow, or at Sellafield's nuclear plant. It was known as 'The Cornflake', because the homes there sold for three times what most people paid locally. So it was thought they could only afford to live on cheap breakfast cereals.

There wasn't much high-street shopping in Millom. Beyond the likes of Bargain Booze, Somerfield, the Co-op and a few small businesses, you were pretty stuck. In the terraced part of town, where me and my dad lived, things

often looked pretty bleak. You could imagine tumble-
weed blowing down the dusty streets, like some forsaken
Western shanty. In heavy winds, squashed Coke cans
flew around like razor blades. And there was an air of
quiet desperation that sometimes turned violent.

'If anything happens in the night,' my dad said, 'just
ignore it. Whatever kicks off in the street, don't go to your
window and look. Don't be seen as a witness.'

You need to meet my dad now – the crazy Randolph
Kindness. I'd lived alone with him since my mum left
(not without good reason) and we rubbed along OK. His
mates called him Randy (also not without good reason),
although Dad preferred to be known as Razzle, or The
Razzler.

He was just over six foot tall. He had a mohican hair-
style, which added several inches to his height. It was a
thick band of hair down the middle, from fringe to back
of neck, with the scalp shaved clean on either side. It often
had a dab of purple or some other colour in it. He also
wore a large pair of tinted shades, whatever the weather.

Dad made a living by cleaning windows, and also
repairing them. Millom did a good trade in smashed
glass, often when the local clan was taking revenge on
someone.

Even up a ladder, with sponge in hand, Dad's ear-
phones were jammed in. He whacked the iPod on so
loud you could always tell from a distance what he was
listening to. He liked classic rock with long guitar solos,

or any noisy stuff like Led Zep, Pink Floyd, Oasis, The Who, Motorhead, The Grateful Dead.

I was never big and brash like The Razzler. I was just Andrew Kindness, a bit short and stodgy, with messy brown hair. I'd been wearing a variety of headgear most of my life because my ears looked funny. Other kids called them 'FA Cup ears', saying they stuck out like the handles on that famous football trophy. They weren't really that bad, but people can be cruel.

Sometimes when I was skating around on Orange Flyer, I'd stand there trapping my ears back with both hands. And my mum knitted me a nice warm hat with long flaps down the sides, which helped to disguise things.

Old ladies thought I was sweet, with my sad brown eyes that once saw too much for a child. And they loved my name, Andrew Kindness, like it somehow implied a saintly soul.

'Just the kind of name you'd like your daughter to marry,' they cooed, like I was still gurgling in a pram.

I thought it a daft name to live up to. And yet another good reason to stay shtoom about my private passion for daffodils. Imagine the grief I'd get from the gang that roamed Millom after dark, looking for anything to stick their boots into. They called themselves the Bronx Crew, which I know is really naff, but they were all related in some way to the bandits who ran this town. Mess with any of the Crew, and wait for your windows to splinter within the hour.

That's why I preferred to keep my own quiet company. And that's just the silent way I might have carried on, but for the strange events of the spring season when I was fifteen.

FIVE

Shortly after I had watched a helpless father and son die, I was called to the official inquest. I was the main witness, but could hardly speak for nerves. The coroner said there was no evidence to suggest foul play. Both man and boy had an excess of sand and water in their lungs, the cause of death. The boy had fifteen kilos of sand in his pants and pockets. These were the cold bare facts, read out in court like sports results.

Six years on from that, when I was fifteen, my life began to turn around. Six years is also an important landmark in the life of a daffodil. When you plant them from seeds, their first green shoots appear above ground after twelve months. And from first seed to full flower normally takes six years of growth. After that, the bulbs below ground keep splitting, like they're making twins of themselves. That's when you can dig them up, leave one bulb where it is, and plant the other elsewhere. But if you plant daffodils from bulbs, and not from seeds, they'll be out in full flower the next year.

Granddad Hebthwaite's tree of Golden Glories still bloomed every spring on that grassy plain facing the bay. The estuary does look lovely with its glittering sands on top. It's the black-grey sludge waiting below that's the real evil. Local newsagents sell tide timetables so you know when to avoid walking out there.

Granddad had moved into a nursing home a few miles away in Ulverston, where Mum lived. He phoned me the week after my fifteenth birthday, sounding urgent and tired.

'Andrew, there is something I must ask of you. There's a little part of the garden here that I'm allowed the use of. Could you bring me a batch of Golden Glory bulbs on your next visit? I'd like to have some flowering nearby.'

'Sure,' I said. 'Where will I get them from?'

'There is only one place,' Granddad said. 'I used up all my own bulbs for that tree-shape I planted six years ago, overlooking the bay. You'll have to dig some of them up and take out the split bulbs.'

I went silent. Dark memories crowded around me like old ghosts. I hadn't gone near that stretch of Duddon's estuary since we first planted those bulbs.

Granddad said, 'Can you do that for me? Can you find the strength to go down there?'

I sucked in deeply and nodded. 'OK,' I said. 'I can try. I'll go tonight.'

'Of course you can. I'll be thinking of you.'

'Thanks, Granddad. Goodnight then.'

'Goodnight, Andy. And always believe in yourself.'

That evening, I had to get through the nightly ritual of supper with my dad first. There was no one downstairs when I skated home around half five. I went upstairs in case The Razzler had crashed out, kicking open his bedroom door and holding my nose.

His room was a right sight. CDs, magazines, plates and ashtrays everywhere. His bedding stank like a pile of steaming hay. Here he rutted and rumbled with any stray damsel of Millom's dark hours. He'd appear some mornings with a strange lady in tow, his eyes blood-red like a sleazy light.

The front door opened, then Dad clanked a bucket that he used for window cleaning.

'Andy?' he shouted. 'You in?'

'Here,' I called back. 'You want me to cook tonight?'

'No need. Been down the chippy.'

I groaned. Yet another night on the fat 'n' gristle. I went downstairs to our slummy kitchen, which hadn't been cleaned properly in the years since Mum left. We hardly ever kept regular supplies of good food now. There were a few jars of pickled onions and pickled eggs, swimming like eyeballs. It was like being in a serial killer's kitchen.

So we lived on takeaways most nights, now that Mum wasn't here to prepare butternut squash stuffed with white miso and millet, followed by her rainbow fruit terrine. We still had the wallchart she'd left pinned up, with a breakdown of my daily dietary needs. 5 PORTIONS OF FRUIT AND VEG A DAY. That's what it said, above frilly drawings of courgettes and oranges.

5 PORTIONS A DAY. I stared at the guilt-tripping poster on the fridge door. Dad was unwrapping mountains of chips and beans, plus two Pukka pies.

'School OK?' asked Dad.

'The usual,' I said. 'I had a salad for lunch, followed by banana fritters.'

'Uh-huh. You want ketchup on your chips?'

'Um, no thanks. Actually, I'm just gonna steam a few leeks. You want some?'

'Leeks? We've got *leeks*?'

'Some of Mum's. Organic ones from her garden.'

'Nah. I'm fine with this.' He buttered thick sliced white bread, and was away into our murky front room to watch a teatime soap opera.

I trimmed Mum's earthy leeks and simmered their green chunks. I tipped them over my pie and chips, then sat at the paper-strewn table in silence.

'Cor! What a beauty!' Dad roared at some girl on the telly. Or maybe he was in love with his chip-shop supper. After the show ended, he got the stereo cranked up and the house throbbed to Pink Floyd's *The Wall*. That was my cue to get Orange Flyer out from under the stairs and skate away into the chilly early March night. It was time to face my enemy estuary again, and fetch some Golden Glory bulbs for Granddad. But first I need to show you my own 'little piece of heaven on earth'.

* * *

A grotty dark alley lay behind our house. It was an old stony path lying between the houses and some wasteland that formed the council tip. The Razzler had built a big garage and workspace at the back edge of the alley. It was a simple building made from white stones, with local grey slate for the roofing. It had a padlock and everything, so he kept his flashy red sports car safely in there.

He loved messing with cars, and people got him to do repairs to their own engines for cash. He had also set up a night class for teenage tearaways, teaching the mechanics of machinery and stuff. Instead of stealing cars, Dad wanted them to value the smooth beauty of a high-class vehicle. Even one or two of the local Bronx Crew wasters took part. This group of Dad's was called the Motor Heads, after one of his favourite bands.

Behind the far end of our garage was my garden space. There was a little door to step through in the garage's back wall. My flowerbeds were only about three metres across, the width of the garage. I was hidden on both sides by high corrugated iron sheets, which Dad put up for my privacy. These sheets filled the gap between the end of our garage to the council tip's electric fence. Beyond my beds of blooming flowers, over the fence, lay a wasteland of rubbish and old junk.

And beyond all that was the coastal railway line that ran through Millom. Sometimes you'd see a cargo of nuclear waste being shunted down from Sellafield. Some of the Bronx Crew would wait for it and pelt the train with stones. It wasn't their protest at the nuclear industry – they just liked to wind up the armed guards on board the nuclear express. Sometimes the guards would aim their machine guns back at the gang, and they weren't fooling about.

I had a padlock key and went into the garage, taking care not to graze Dad's car. It was a bright red, low-slung thing, with an open-top roof. Stacked around it were various ladders, pots, tools and cloths for his window-cleaning work. I unbolted a latch at the end and went through to my own private paradise.

Six

OK, so here's how daffodils work. The head of each flower has a ring of petals (the perianth), and inside these is a trumpet shape. This contains a stem called the stigma, and a pod below it called the ovary.

And here's what happens when the natural world gets kinky. When bees or insects go inside the flower's trumpet, they collect pollen on their bodies. The bees are after a taste of something sweet that also smells exotic. So then they brush against the daffodil's stigma (that's the sticky-out bit), leaving the pollen. The pollen travels down the stigma into the ovary (the seed pod). This fertilizes the seeds already there.

When the pod bursts open, the seeds are scattered onto the earth below. From then on they can start to grow. So simple. The male and female parts all in one! No endless courting, dating, or weeping into your pillow over the diamond girl in Year Eleven. But daffs are just as wild and lusty as us. And each seed produces a unique offspring.

I checked the progress of a new species I was crossbreeding. Three years in, and promising green shoots were pushing through the soil. Three more years to full flowering glory. I stuffed a plastic bag in my jeans, pulled on the flappy wool hat, got a trowel and skated through dusky Millom. But as I rolled along Dayton Street, where I lived, a load of the Bronx Crew came stumbling out of the night towards me.

We'd always shared an uneasy peace, them and me. I was vaguely cool, on account of the skateboard thing and my occasional use of the skate slopes behind Somerfield supermarket. But they sensed I was different, in the way that animals can sense the approach of an unknown species.

The Bronx Crewers were aged from about fourteen to eighteen, all dressed in tracksuits, white caps and trainers. That evening they'd probably been getting wasted down at Little Copse. It was on the far side of the bay, where a red dirt track ran down through bumpy fields. A farm gate had been smashed to allow car access for lazy druggies. A circle of bricks marked a campfire site where the Crew gathered.

I tried not to catch anyone's eye, but some youth stuck out a hand as I passed. His chalky face was white like his cap. It was Jason Brindley.

'All reet, Big Ears?' he shouted. 'Keep away from the bay! It's a *killer*!'

I skated on, heart stomping and tears of guilt rising. It didn't take much to loosen them, even six years on.

'Leave him be,' came a girl's voice. 'Diana fancies him.'

'Do not!'

'You so do.'

'Do *not!*'

I was out of earshot, kicking the ground to increase my speed. Diana must be Diana Dowder, with her ginger hair and big lumpy body. I felt my own stigma stirring within my baggy jeans. The interest of any girl, chav or cheerleader, was enough to get this boy's pollen flying. Diana was a bit grisly, but so was I. You take what's there.

I veered left off a quiet lane and made for the spooky slag bank facing the dark bay. It's also known as The Slaggy. Back in the mining days, they used to deposit debris from the iron ore just here. Loads of white-hot rocks were left lying, and their ashy colour hasn't changed over the years.

As I skated across the rocky heights, a big moon hung above. Its reflection rippled whitely in the estuary water. On bright nights The Slaggy glowed like a lunar landscape. And it's weird how people were always losing things around there. Frisbees, footballs, you name it. It's like the earth just swallowed them up. And when you looked at the ground, it was like walking on the moon.

With my knees bent, I steered Orange Flyer down the steep bank. Then it was over a stretch of cracked marshland, up to the grassy scrub where Granddad's tree of daffodils lay. All those Golden Glories gleamed like warm lamps in the night.

I stared out at the waterlogged bay beyond with a

violent shudder, as the scenes of years before came in rapid flashback. I sat with knees tucked up, my head resting there. My forearms covered my eyes, but nothing could halt the total recall. I leaped up with a gasp, feeling the presence of a sickly boy and his balding dad.

But I was alone in the night, and quickly got busy with a trowel. Out came several flowers in that tree-shape as I pulled away the extra bulbs each one had made below. Then I replanted those with flowers growing and packed the soil back around them. They'd bloom away just like before.

It was nearly ten o'clock by the time I'd done, and my messy hair sweated under Mum's hat. I lay and rested for a bit, trying to flatten my ears through the woolly flaps. I hauled myself up to The Slaggy, and lay on rocky white-ness looking up at the moon.

I was just about to step onto Orange Flyer when a car crawled into view below. I was on the raised and gleam-ing embankment, the dark bay and mountain ranges behind me.

The car's headlights cut out. I lay on the cool slag bank and peered into the gloom. Two people got out of the car. I saw orange cigarette pinpricks. Voices carried up to me, one male, one female.

'You at college tomorrow?' asked the man.

'What? Oh, sure, about nine,' replied the young woman. She sounded familiar. I strained to see, but both were wearing dark clothes.

The man raised his voice. 'Don't be a slave to the system. Don't let 'em grind you down, baby!' It was the kind of empty slogan my dad spouted.

'I won't!' the girl shouted. 'I belong to nobody!' She whirled around, arms aloft.

'Hey! *I'm* not a nobody!' shouted the guy, pulling her close. 'I'm a big voice in these parts.'

They both giggled and embraced, and started pawing each other. Then they hustled back into the car, which began gently rocking a few minutes later. I sat and stared and imagined. Then I lay back and gazed at the bright moon. At some point I must have dozed off. The car was pulling away, and the girl went skipping along after it.

In my drowsed state, sitting up clumsily, I shifted some rocks. As the girl looked up to her right, the moonlight caught her full on. She lifted a hand to shield her eyes. I flopped back down.

'Who's there?' she called out. 'Friend or foe?'

I lay there, dead still and breathless.

'Hello?' she sang. 'Hello-*oh*? That you, Martha? You making out with Stevo?'

Martha must be Martha Tinker. A willowy angel, with hair dyed alternate blocks of blonde and dark red. She had the cutest ears ever, like a sweet mouse.

'OK, well don't forget,' said the girl below. 'No naughty stuff. Remember Lauren Todd? One kid baked, another in the cooker.' And she danced away in the car's fumy trail, off towards the newer Cornflake estate on the far side of Millom. I eased my head up and watched her leggy figure depart. She tugged off a shiny leather jacket and stuffed it in her holdall.

I shook my head in wonder. It was Angela Hutchinson! *Angie Hutch!* The dead brainy girl most likely to leave Millom and never return. A year above me at school, but so far beyond me we lived in opposite universes. Angie Hutch, who won a prize for something scholarly every term. Who once read her award-winning poetry to royalty when they crawled up to south Cumbria. And here she was out in the night, acting like some wild floozy from the Bronx Crew.

It seemed like spring fever was rising in Millom, for sure. I felt its sweet heat inside me for the second time that evening.

SEVEN

I rarely went to the school library. What with my grand-dad's daffodil books and my school homework, I had enough reading material. But next lunch time I went up to the library, knowing I'd be sure to catch Angela Hutchinson. I wanted proof that the loud nymphet I'd seen in the dark last night was the swotty scholar I'd always imagined.

In fact, it was one of the days she helped the librarian. Angie was in the lower sixth form, but she often seemed to be running the school. She carried armfuls of books about, tidied shelves and showed dozy Year Sevens where to find kiddy comics.

I sat down, pretending to read, and studied Angie. She was tall, graceful and very leggy. She wore an old-fashioned school blazer, all blue and black pinstripes. Her hair was a luscious strawberry-blonde – not quite yellow, not yet reddish. She also had the kind of tiny round specs that bossy academics wear on TV. And those leggy legs were bare except for white ankle socks. Her limbs flashed under a short grey skirt. She looked down and caught me staring. 'Can I help?' she asked politely.

'I'm fine.' I blushed, staring down at some classic novel.

'OK. Well, sing out if you need anything. I'm all yours.'

I squirmed, peeping at those legs when Angie's slender back was turned. *I'm all yours.* Was that a sign? I knew it wasn't.

Elbows on the table, I stared at pages of text without reading a word. And I covered my FA Cup ears in misery.

Daffodils were sprouting up everywhere in Millom that day. Many of them were of my granddad's doing, in private, down the years. He'd never blown his own trumpet about his talent. And I kept quiet in case I got laughed at for messing with flowers.

But there was one special display that I'd planted from bulbs, the year before I turned fifteen. So I couldn't wait to check it out in full bloom. And here's why.

In my final term at junior school we'd gone off on a coach trip to Grasmere. We went to visit Dove Cottage, where the poet William Wordsworth lived. You know, the guy who wrote, *I wandered lonely as a cloud*, and whatnot. It's actually a poem which mentions daffodils, but I'll save all that for later.

We were guided around the damp and cold cottage by some girl with a German accent. We all got giggly at her strange voice, and then at the small four-poster bed where William slept. And we went even dafter in the room where all his various hash pipes were kept. I know we were only ten or eleven years old at the time, but in Millom there's certain things you know about from the cradle.

He didn't have a bad life, that Wordsworth. He got his long-suffering sister to write up all his notes, while he lounged around with Coleridge smoking pot. I mean, I'm not saying he wasn't a great poet, but a druggie is still a druggie in any century.

Anyhow, on the way home I had a major disaster. I had been nervous all day, without my skateboard and being away from Millom. I'd never left the place before, except on car trips here and there. I even took Orange Flyer on those journeys.

Being nervous made my throat dry, so I drank loads of water and orange squash. I kept seeing the pavements of Grasmere village dissolve into quicksand. All the drink I'd kept for the journey home had been drunk by the time we boarded the bus back.

Many of Cumbria's roads are hardly fit for vehicles. They're rutted and ragged and twist like mad. My bladder was at bursting point before we'd got to Ambleside. Luckily, no one had sat next to me. I was still seen as an oddity with big ears who had witnessed death and disaster two years before.

Twisting my body next to the window, I fumbled down my trouser zip for my thingy. I had a quick bursting pee into a plastic Co-op bag. I stuffed the hot and wet carrier into my small rucksack. But it was quite old, and its corners were jagged where the lining poked through. And those sharp edges pierced the Co-op bag, which already had some air holes in to stop daft little kids from suffocating. So out through a corner of the rucksack leaked my fresh wazz.

I wasn't even aware until a pool of orange lay under my seat. I looked down in horror. I'd never live this down in Millom. As the bus lurched around another corkscrew corner, my urine seeped into the gangway.

'Ugh! Someone's wet themselves!' shouted a kid across the aisle.

'Where? *Where?* Who? *Who?*' came the excited cries.

Mrs Tyson, with her fiery voice, sat right behind me. As soon as she realized what was happening, she got the driver to stop. Instead of making me look stupid, she ordered everyone off to stretch their legs in a field. And then she set about cleaning my bag with tissue paper, tipping my piddle into her own coffee flask and wiping the floor. All this took place with me off the coach, watching through the window.

By the time we got back on, there was no orange puddle any more. My Co-op bag was binned, my rucksack dried and Mrs Tyson's thermos tightly closed.

Mrs Tyson shouted, 'Somebody's container of orange squash came undone. Please be more careful, children. Screw the tops on tightly.'

The whole class groaned. Nothing more shocking than a burst bottle.

Mrs Tyson whispered to me, 'I think *you* need a new rucksack. I may have a spare one at home, from my hiking group.'

I was so grateful for her kindness that I travelled back vowing to repay her one day. And then, in the spring when I was fourteen, I heard that Mrs Tyson's husband had died suddenly. They'd lived together in Millom, and her husband was big on the local charity scene. He also looked after the local nature reserves, and was close friends with my granddad.

And so, shortly after Mr Tyson was buried, I gathered some of Granddad's Mystic daffodil bulbs. This was a species he'd cross-bred from the Moina and Merlin varieties. In full flower, they had large yellow petals, so broad they overlapped. And the trumpet part was ringed with bright red.

I'd gone down to Mr Tyson's grave in the town churchyard. The cemetery sloped and rolled in green waves. And in the darkness I got busy, knowing that a floral work of art would be created if this pattern worked well.

So by the time I was fifteen, a year later, I couldn't wait to see how the display had turned out. I skated to the church after school, the same day I'd spied on Angie Hutch in the library. I got off Orange Flyer and walked on gravel between the tombs. Skating among the dead wasn't something that felt decent.

I stopped a little way off. Mrs Tyson, short and grey,

stood by her husband's grave. With her were two other ladies, both quite frail and holding walking sticks. I could hear quiet weeping from where I lurked by an old headstone.

'It's just so . . . astonishing!' said Mrs Tyson, a hanky to her eyes.

'It really is, Margaret,' said one of the old birds. She wore a pink cardigan and a chunky pearl necklace. 'It's nothing less than an act of mercy.'

'Truly an act of God's will,' said the third one, in a tartan dress.

Mrs Tyson nodded her blunt and ashy head. 'I believe so,' she said, still sobbing gently. 'How else could flowers arrange themselves like this?'

It was what they wanted to believe, and who could deny them such faith? I drifted quietly away, and waited in the chilly church until they'd gone. Then I crept over to Mr Tyson's grave as the afternoon darkened. The church clock boomed six times. Nobody else was about.

Even though the planting from bulbs was done in the dark a year ago, I had to admire the pattern I'd made. Granddad's vivid Mystic daffodils stood in the perfect shape of a heart. It lay right by the grave, about a metre across. Broad buttery petals gave off an almost holy glow. The vivid red ring inside them seemed like the blood of Christ. I stared at this garden Valentine I'd created. I shivered at the simple power of nature to cover itself in such glory.

I made a mental note to borrow Dad's mobile, with its camera, and take some snaps for Granddad. A sight like this would soon pick him up. I walked away from that red-gold heart of daffodils, feeling so proud and pleased.

EIGHT

Back in Millom early that evening, I skated onto Lapstone Road, where the Co-op was still open. Classical music belted out of speakers above the entrance. It was done to keep crowds of kids from hanging around there, but most of them wore iPods and couldn't hear the rousing string symphony.

At the top of our street stood a grubby bookie's. The windows were filled with placards offering wild bets on football and racing results. As I trundled by the bookie's, its door burst open. Out came Long John McKay, a tough Scots guy nearly seven foot tall. A fist sprang from the dark doorway and sent McKay sprawling. Only one guy in England's north-west could take Long John apart like this.

Malcolm Dowder, snug in a suede coat, followed Long John into the street. He booted the fallen skinhead on the knee, then stood over his victim.

Malcolm's voice had a hint of squeaky Scouser. 'Like I said,' he told John, 'I think you'll find it *was* Irish Dandy what won the Derby last year. Check your facts, mate.'

As Long John lay and cursed, Malcolm Dowder went back inside, banging the door. I kicked the ground and skated on home. All that aggro over a stupid horse race.

OK, so it's time to meet Malcolm 'Malky' Dowder. He was known in private as 'Talcum Powder', though say that in his earshot and prepare to eat dirt off the pavement. I reckon he was fifty-odd back then; you couldn't picture him as a child. His forehead was large and craggy, and what dark hair was left on top got swept back with a lick. His right eye was quite bozzy, its pupil rolling away from the nose, so you made sure to look him in the left one. He wore big sheepskin or suede coats, tight white trousers and cowboy boots.

Whatever happened in Millom always got back to him. Half the women in our part of town had kids with Malky, and their daughters bred with his sons, and so on. Diana Dowder was one of Malky's many offspring, which had made it slightly scary when I'd overheard she might like me.

'Leave him be . . . Diana fancies him.'

'Do not!'

'You so do.'

Even that was sweet music to my FA Cup ears. For me, it was close to a declaration of undying love.

Back at home, The Razzler excelled himself over supper. Fried black pudding (made from pigs' blood), with a bacon muffin and mushy peas. All washed down with a four-pack of Stella.

'Had a right drag of a day,' Dad moaned, stirring

ancient mint sauce into the peas. 'Repaired some smashed house windows on the Cornflake. This posh bloke must've offended Malky or one of his clan. You want any black pud?'

'Er . . . no.' I hacked ice from our freezer compartment and found a soggy pack of veggie burgers. 'I'll have these with leeks and beans.'

'Suit yourself. I've got the Motor Heads coming round in a bit. Gonna show them how to fit new spark plugs. What you up to later?'

I topped and tailed the last of Mum's organic veg. 'Not much. Might join your group for a bit,' I said. 'Um, I don't suppose a girl called Diana ever tags along, does she?'

'Diana Dowder? She's one of Malky's brood. Can't remember who the mother is. Anyway, don't go messing with the clan, Andy. Not unless you're gonna get hitched. You fancy her?'

I reddened and laughed. 'No way. Don't even know her.'

'She's been along once or twice, just to hang out. Big girl. Why the interest?'

'No reason. It's nothing.'

At half past seven, assorted Millom youths hung loose in our back alley. Dad opened the garage and pulled out an old car engine. As he talked technical bits to the group, they listened and crouched and smoked. The idea was that the Motor Heads would put together their own vehicle from scratch, using spare bits bought off scrap dealers. First, they all needed some lessons in the basics.

An hour later, when everyone was getting greasy, a woman called by. It was Mrs Hutchinson, Angie's mum and an important Voice of the Village. She also held the post of High Sheriff of Cumbria. This was mainly a ceremonial role, escorting high court judges, attending royal visits, working with young offenders.

Mrs Hutchinson called on Dad every month for any news titbit she could feed into her weekly local paper column. I could've told her plenty about what was really going on, but Ethel Hutchinson was more concerned with traditional matters. To read her column, you'd think the whole of Millom was having tea party fund-raisers for a teddy bears' picnic.

A middle-aged woman who seemed set on looking antique, she wore a white cardigan and brown tights. Her hair was curled and silvery, and her glasses were thickly metallic. She approached the swearing and sweaty group, where Dad lay under his red sports car. Only his purple mohican haircut was visible.

'Good evening, Mr Kindness,' she said, bending and creaking.

Dad slid out. 'Ah . . . Ma Hutch. You really must learn to call me Randy.'

She tittered politely. 'I wonder, Mr Kindness, if you have any news to share with the community? I gather your group of little mechanics here has stirring plans.'

One of the little mechanics giggled, and passed around a bottle of Jack Daniels.

'Oh, for sure,' said Dad, sitting up. He eyed Mrs Hutchinson through his square tinted shades. 'Tony over there has just got back from a six-month young offender's stretch. He's planning to go straight until Christmas. That right, Tone?'

'That's about it, Razzle.'

Mrs Hutchinson smoothed her woolly cardie. 'Yes, that's very stirring,' she said. 'I wonder if you have any news that is a little more . . . cosy? Or comforting?'

Dad knew what she was after, but couldn't resist tormenting. He sat in the stony alley, tapping his teeth. Finally he gave in and said, 'Oh, yeah. There is something. We've received a grant from Rural Enterprise to fund this project into next year. By which time there should be a home-made Motor Heads car doing ninety around the bends. That right, crew?'

Six voices chorused their agreement. Mrs Hutchinson whipped out a notepad and took down the details. I was lurking by the gate of our little backyard, and she turned her gaze on me.

'Good evening, Andrew.'

'Hello. How's Angie?'

'Angela is *very* well, thank you. We have just heard that one of her poems is among the winners in this year's Cumbrian Teenage Writers awards. This follows her previous wins at a national level, in various under-sixteen groups.'

'That's good,' I said. I thought of her running wild with some bloke near The Slaggy last night. I thought of him shouting, 'Don't be a slave to the system! Don't let them grind you down, girl.' I thought of his car rocking about with Angie inside it.

I said, 'It must keep Angie dead busy, all this writing.'

'Indeed it does.' The proud mother beamed. 'Just last night she was running a reading group for junior children in the library. She refused to let me attend, saying any adults would ruin the children's attention. And she got back so late, what with cleaning up afterwards. But now I must go, before I ruin the attention of your father's engineering students. Goodnight, Andrew. Goodnight, Mr Kindness, and thank you.'

NINE

Diana Dowder had been excluded from school for a while. Something to do with riding her bicycle into maths, waving a bra at the teacher. I saw her come back one morning. Wobbly bottom, short ginger hair. She was chewing gum from side to side like a cow chews cud, and gave me a clumsy wink. Her thick tongue stuck out at the same time.

In assembly, the headmistress followed up on what Angie's mum had recently told me.

'We are delighted to announce that Angela Hutchinson is among the winners in this year's Cumbrian Teenage Writers competition. Her poem will be on display in the library from lunch time.'

I popped upstairs later to read it. I didn't quite get the gist of it. The poem had lots of images to do with war crimes and foreign cheeses. I think I got that much right.

A boy from my class saw me peering at the poem. 'Angie Hutchinson?' he sneered. 'Total posh breezy, Andy. And she's older than you. And taller. And smarter. And—'

'Shut up,' I said. 'I'm trying to understand what she's written. Is there a war going on in a place called Brie?'

* * *

That evening I fell onto the sofa after Dad's hearty supper of chicken wings and fried potatoes. I glanced at my watch. Nearly nine o'clock, and time for *The Rock Show* on Bay Radio.

It was our Friday ritual, Dad and me, to listen to DJ Terry Tilson from nine till eleven. Bay Radio was the region's independent station, and Terry knocked out some top tunes for two hours, twice a week. I flicked on the stereo as Terry was welcoming us to 'another mad night of melody and mayhem'.

We listened and nodded along, sometimes writing down a new band's name. Terry put on this deepish voice for the radio that you could tell was false. Near the end of the show I was lying down and drifting off. Dad's eyes were closed and he was starting to belch rather loudly. Terry began to wind things up for the night. He mentioned a few local gigs, gave the show's website and signed off.

'And remember, kids,' he drawled deeply. *'Don't be a slave to the system. Don't let them grind you down, guys.* Stay true to your rock-and-roll roots. This is DJ Terry Tilson for Bay Radio. Sleep easy.'

I sat up sharply and stared at the stereo. I'd been so stunned to hear Angie in the darkness the other night that the man's voice had passed me by. I knew it had sounded familiar. The slogans Terry had just spouted were the same ones I'd heard that night. Same accent too.

I rubbed my head in sleepy shock. Well, what a

stunner! Angie Hutchinson, poetic daughter of the High Sheriff of Cumbria, was getting it on with a rock DJ maybe twice her age. And there was me thinking that I lived some sort of double life.

'Wassup?' said Dad, standing and yawning. 'You dreaming about Diana Dowder?'

'No,' I said, lying down with a sigh. 'Not dreaming of her at all.'

The Razzler's breakfast on a Saturday morning was something to behold. Most weekdays he was up early, taking just black coffee and leftover pizza before going off on his window-cleaning rounds. Sometimes it was two fried eggs and a dry Martini. But at the weekend he indulged fully. He called this brekky fest 'The Works'. It consisted of poached eggs, baked beans, spicy pork sausages fried in lard, grilled bacon and thickly buttered white toast. He sat down to scoff, moaning with joy like something kinky was going on. He squirted ketchup over this and that on the vast plate.

Our kitchen walls ran with grease. All the windows were open. Dad used to be a vegetarian because Mum was too, and she did all the cooking. He spent his evenings back then in the garage, or even going out for a jog. After Mum left, he stopped being veggie, got lazy and had Sky TV installed. It was like he was trying to get at her somehow, to pay her back for leaving, even though he'd only got himself to blame.

The Saturday after DJ Terry exposed his little secret to me on air, I went over to Mum's in Ulverston. She's a funny one, my mother. She and Dad got together through Cumbria's alternative lifestyle scene, which wasn't exactly big, so you knew pretty much everyone in it.

They were both travellers, truth-seekers, dropouts. They set up a little catering van, which went round all the green festivals doing veggie grub. My mum did the cooking and Dad sorted out the mechanics. They moved to Millom, where my dad comes from, and Mum got work in a health-food shop in Ulverston. Dad stayed out of the mainstream, setting up as a window cleaner and odd jobber.

'Anything to beat the bow and scrape of a nine-to-five,' he told me. So they both stayed close to their radical roots, with a bit of normality added in the shape of a terraced house. And then . . . me!

But my dad wasn't known as Randy for nothing. If Mum suspected he had casual flings and affairs, she stayed quiet long enough. But when I was twelve, three years after the bay tragedy I witnessed, The Razzler pushed his luck.

He hadn't come home for his lunch one day, like normal. Mum went out in search of him, in case he'd had an accident. She scouted around the small town until she found his ladder leaning against some house a few rows away. No sign of my dad.

Mum climbed the ladder, surely knowing what she'd

find. She got to the top and peeked in through a closed, freshly washed window. And there was Dad, smoking in bed with a buxom Irish lady called Maggie Maguire.

'Such a dull cliché,' Mum once said. 'The naughty window cleaner, like something from an old black-and-white movie.'

After all that, Mum scrapped her plans for more children with Randy, had a bit of a breakdown and moved round the coast to Ulverston. She suffered from depression, and once took too many prescription pills, which landed her in hospital. So she wasn't in a fit state to look after me, and I was settled at secondary school in Millom by then, with Granddad Hebthwaite also living nearby. His wife, Grandma Hebthwaite, had died suddenly when I was five. It was some years later, after I left junior school, that Granddad's health got worse and he needed regular care. So he went into a nursing home a short drive from Mum's.

Now and then Mum would ask if I'd like to go and live with her in Ulverston. I felt tempted sometimes, now that she was coping better with life. But her mania for wholesome food could get just as tiring as Dad's junk diet. And at least with The Razzler I had more freedom to come and go, without endless questions about what I'd been up to. So I stayed put in Millom, and headed for Mum's at the weekends.

I took Orange Flyer on the midday bus to Ulverston. It's a small market town just down the coast that also has an open bay. Mum's health food shop, called Grass Roots, was at the end of a cobbled shopping street. Among the lentils and organic flapjacks was a vast array of natural pills and potions.

Mum had learned about everything weird and wonderful down the years. She had studied haiku, Urdu, Hebrew, hoodoo, voodoo, jujitsu, shiatsu, feverfew, sudoku, smoked tofu, and cock-a-doodle-doo for all I knew. I missed her, and I missed her cooking, even if some of it was a bit manic. I remembered having Wild Rice and Corn Loaf with Bulgur Walnut Croquettes one Christmas Day, while Millom town smelled of turkey 'n' roast spuds.

She was short and stocky like me, with jet-black hair. Her chin was pierced with a flashy stud, and she wore darkly gothic clothes. There was always a long skirt, ankle-length, like something from centuries back.

I popped into Grass Roots and got a kiss that left a chin-stud dent in my cheek. Then I skated uphill out of town to the care home. I had a bag of Golden Glory bulbs for Granddad. The day was bright and mild.

The care home was off the main road, down a long private path. It was like some old stately house converted into little rooms. I rang the doorbell and let myself in, as the staff all knew me.

'Hello, Andrew,' said a woman in a starchy white outfit. 'Come to see Granddad?'

'Yeah. Is he out in the garden?'

She stopped and sighed. 'No, I'm afraid not. He's had a bit of a relapse. He's resting in bed just now.'

I raced around her and upstairs to Granddad's room. He lay in pyjamas, silvery head back on the pillows, breathing deeply. His black-rimmed glasses were on the bedside table, by a glass of water and bottles of pills.

'Hello, there,' he said with a wheeze.

'Granddad! What's wrong?'

'Oh, just a few decades of iron dust clogging me up. And today is your grandma's birthday. Or it would have been if she were still here. I just need to rest, and remember.'

I sat on the bed. 'I'm sorry. But look, I've brought some Golden Glories. I went back to the bay and dug them up at night.'

He breathed heavily. 'So you went back there and faced your demons? Just for me? Well done, Andy. I wondered if you would.'

I played with an earthy bulb. 'It was a dark night,' I said. 'But I could still imagine everything again.'

'It'll fade,' said Granddad. 'You've taken one leap of faith to visit there. And in time you'll be ready to set foot on the sands again.'

I shook my head in doubt. 'Can't you get up?' I asked. 'We can go and plant these Glories. It's nice out.'

'Not today,' said Granddad. 'Not for a while. Why don't you plant them for me?'

I felt gloomy, despite the spring sunlight filling that

little room. Granddad's flowerbeds were under his window, two storeys down.

'I'll be right below you,' I said. 'Open the window and I can shout up.'

'All right.' Granddad smiled. 'And listen ... before you go, it's high time I gave you something. I may never use it again.'

He leaned stiffly across and reached under his bed. With a gasp, he sat back and held out a strange tool. It was like a gigantic corkscrew. An old wooden handle, as long as my forearm, had a metal stalk coming out of it. This ended in a series of twists, with a very sharp point at the end.

'What is it?' I asked, stroking the smooth wooden grip.

'It's called a scutcher,' said Granddad. 'I worked with it down the iron mines, years ago. It was used for taking iron samples from the ore. And we also used it for digging holes in the ore, to place the sticks of dynamite in.'

'Wow,' I said. 'But what can I do with it now?'

Granddad leaned forward with a gasp and took the scutcher from me. 'We often got poor wages as miners,' he said. 'And many of us had gardens or allotments that we worked on too, in our free time. So we used tools from the mines for digging and planting. And this scutcher was perfect for drilling deep holes in the earth, to place my little daffodil bulbs or seeds in.'

'Thank you,' I said. 'I'll treasure it. I promise.'

We sat and chatted a bit longer until Granddad's eyes closed. Then I left quietly and went down to his little garden area. I speared into his flowerbeds with the scutcher, turning its huge corkscrew handle like I was opening a barrel of wine. I made enough small holes to plant a dozen Golden Glories. All around me, various old folk shuffled by in dressing gowns, or stood talking quietly to themselves.

I felt the solemn weight of the scutcher. How many other hands had held this tool over the years? How many iron miners, all working six days a week, ten hours a day, the rims of their hard hats holding little candles to light their way? I thought of my granddad down there in the dirty darkness, his lungs slowly filling with red iron dust. Then back home to a quiet garden, among the gold and the green, the pink and the white of his many daffodils.

Before leaving, I looked up to the open window two levels above. I cupped both hands around my mouth and shouted, 'I love you, Granddad! Get well soon!'

TEN

In a quiet street just out of Ulverston's small town centre, I let myself into Mum's house. Its outer walls were stony white and craggy, and there was a big garden round the back. Rows of vegetables, grown to strict organic standards, lay planted. My mum was Granddad Hebthwaite's daughter, and green fingers ran in their family.

In the living room was Mum's big collection of herbal books and feminist novels. She was also part of an allotment scheme that grew organic herbs to sell as natural remedies, processed into liquid form. Little dark brown bottles and plastic tubs of strange potions took up the floor space. She also brewed big cartons of home-made wine. I looked at the label on what I thought was one of these. It read, DAMIANA.

It must be a fruit I hadn't heard of before. I lifted the lid and sniffed. It smelled a bit iffy, but most of Mum's wines did. I filled a wine glass with Damiana and had a good glug. Yeeuch! It tasted like tea that's been stewing for all eternity. It must be a vat of herbal tincture that had got mixed up with the wine tubs.

I looked up Damiana in one of Mum's guides. The entry read:

Damiana (*Turnera diffusa*). Has a long use in herbal medicine as a mood enhancer. Research shows that parts of this herb produce activity like testosterone. For these reasons, Damiana is often known as the 'sex drive' herb. It can increase sexual pleasure in both males and females. Only use for children under the advice of a herbalist.

I lifted the lid on the tub again to see the dark brown solution inside. Wow, the 'sex drive' herb! Even though it tasted rotten, I stole a jam jar full and hid it in my small rucksack. You never knew in life what might be needed.

Strewn over Mum's kitchen table were several magazines. As I sat and ate organic cheddar from the fridge, I glanced at them. Each mag had the word SKYROS on the front in white letters. Flicking through, I saw photos of some idyllic island surrounded by royal-blue seas. Happy hippy types were strumming acoustic guitars, doing t'ai chi with weird gestures, tucking into outdoor buffets, dancing in the sea surf or strolling on sunlit cobbles.

It seemed as if this Skyros place was a haven for types like my mum. I worked out it was somewhere in the Med, and ran courses all year on yoga, meditation, writing, singing, painting, you name it. Maybe Mum was planning a holiday. I lingered over a photo of some blonde babe getting a mostly naked massage. Sunlight glowed on her glossy bare bum. My fingers began to fidget in my pockets.

Then the front door opened and Mum came in. I stood up, feeling an arousal stick out like a codpiece in my jeans. That Damiana 'sex drive' herbal stuff didn't hang about. I sat down again, hiding my lower half under the table.

'Hello, love,' said Mum, laden down with bags. 'Grab some of these, will you?'

I tried reaching across the table for the heavy carriers.

'Quick!' shouted Mum. 'I'm gonna drop them.'

I ran round, doubling up like someone in agony to hide my swelling. I took two bags and crouched back to the table, sitting down sharply.

'Andy?' said Mum. 'You ill?'

'Bit of a stomach ache.'

'Really? That'll be your dad's junk food. I'll make you some fennel and turmeric tea.'

'Oh, no, don't worry. It's easing off now.'

'You sure?'

'*Dead* sure. How was work?'

'A busy Saturday. How's your granddad?'

I crossed my legs, not very easily, as Mum came by. 'It's hard to say. He's in bed mostly now.'

Mum sighed. 'So the nurse said when I phoned last night. I'll go there tomorrow. You staying over?'

'Aye. What's for tea?'

'Home-made pizza.'

'Yeah? Great.'

'Though if your tummy's playing up, maybe I'll leave off the cheese. Put some smoked tofu on instead.'

'Oh. You needn't. Don't deprive yourself for me.'

'The tofu's better for you anyway. Be ready in half an hour.

Over supper, at which I was allowed an organic lager, we chatted like old mates.

'So, how's life in mad Millom?' asked Mum.

'Same as ever. Angie Hutchinson's won another teen prize for her writing.'

Mum slurped some of her cherry wine, which looked and smelled like Damiana. 'She was always brainy. And real bonny. A year older than you, yeah?'

'Yeah. And she's still brainy and bonny.' I heard a note of misery in my voice.

Mum touched my hand. 'There'll be someone for you. No need to rush at fifteen.'

'Don't matter if I rush or not. No one's ever gonna love Mr FA Cup Ears.'

Mum dumped some more leafy salad on my plate. 'Oh, they'll flatten out in time. We've all got something about our looks that we hate. Change what you can and accept what you can't. Learn to love yourself a bit more, or nobody else ever will.'

'What is there to love?' I asked. 'I've got no real friends. I've got a sad hobby with daffodils that only my family knows about. I'm a bit short and chubby and once watched two innocent people die. Try writing a Lonely Hearts ad out of that lot.'

Mum pointed a fork at me. 'That's enough,' she said sharply. 'You need some help in gaining more self-esteem. And in letting go of anxiety. But I've got some ideas on that front. I'll let you know before long what I think we might try. It could change your life.'

ELEVEN

My life really did begin to turn cartwheels that next week. And it all kicked off when Angie Hutchinson pushed her luck too far, one school day afternoon.

Giving the excuse that she had a dentist appointment in Ulverston, Angie took the lunchtime train out of Millom. On reaching Ulverston, she darted into the public toilets behind the town hall. There she stripped out of her school clothes, and put on tight jeans, tank top and leather jacket. In the dark and grotty loos she applied eyeliner, lipstick and blusher.

At half past two Angie met someone in the town centre. His light-brown hair was brushed back and thinning a bit. The sides were shaved close. He had a beard growing under his chin, which was almost square. He wore baggy jeans with big pockets and a dark hooded jacket. Over one shoulder he carried a black holdall bulging with CDs, posters and vinyl.

It was DJ Terry Tilson, from Bay Radio. He was waiting by the war memorial at the top of the cobbled market street. Also at half past two, our school's deputy headmaster left the optician's just by the memorial. Suffering with severe headaches, Mr Hillman had been given leave that afternoon for a meeting with his eye consultant.

He could hardly believe that Angela Hutchinson was hanging out in town. The poetic librarian and prize scholar, dressed like a raunchy rocker when she should be in double English. Mr Hillman donned some dark glasses, as advised by the optician to help his headaches, and followed. A small man, with a moony plain face, he didn't stick out in crowds.

Angie and Terry went into the Farmer's Arms, a pub that looks down on the bustling market street. Mr Hillman followed, still unsure if this really was Angie holding hands with what looked like a drug dealer. As the couple found a corner table, Mr Hillman spied on them from the next bar.

Finally he texted the headmistress, asking if she could check on Angie's whereabouts. When a text came back saying she was at the dentist's, Mr Hillman finished his lemonade and left by a side entrance.

Next morning, at break, Angie was called to the head-mistress's office. There was nothing unusual in that. She thought it was something to do with World Book Day. Maybe Mrs Longden wanted Angie to organize an event for the Year Sevens.

She knocked on the door and was summoned in. Mrs Longden sat sternly behind her desk, with Mr Hillman to one side. The school librarian, Mr Reardon, was there too.

Still nothing to be wary of, she thought. Perhaps they wanted her to promote the school's new Learning Zone when she collected an award at the Cumbrian Teenage Writers night.

She wasn't kept in suspense for long. Mrs Longden sat with fingers steepled under her chin. Her heavily lined face spoke of decades battling the education system.

'Angela,' she said quietly, 'can you just confirm where you were yesterday afternoon? Only I have a typed letter here stating you were due to attend the dentist.'

Angie's face looked washed out. She toyed with her strawberry-blonde locks. Maybe her leggy legs quaked a little. She knew the game was up.

'I faked the letter,' she said softly. 'I met someone in town. As I'm sure you know.'

'Yes, we know,' said Mrs Longden. 'And we are not best pleased. If word of this was to leak out, can you imagine what example it would set to the younger children? They look up to you as a role model ... as a shining light in this little town.'

'I'm very sorry, Mrs Longden. It won't happen again.'

'Indeed it will *not*!' shouted Mrs Longden. She sat back, with shelves of leathery books behind her. Angie got nervous and crossed her legs. Very slowly, she rubbed her left shoe up her bare right shin. Mr Hillman and Mr Reardon tried hard not to watch.

'In normal circumstances, you would face exclusion at this point. Your family would certainly be informed too. We might even involve the police, given the obvious age difference between yourself, a schoolgirl, and your companion yesterday.'

Angie whispered, 'Please, no. Leave Terry out of this.'

Mrs Longden gave no sign that she'd heard. 'However,' she said, 'we have a task in mind, which I trust will occupy your many creative talents. It should also keep you too busy to ever consider flouting the school's rules again. You may sit down.'

Angie took a chair. She sat cross-legged, her short grey skirt rising to offer a flash of orange knickers. Mr Hillman tried hard not to notice. Mr Reardon, his beard striped like a badger, closed his eyes.

'A few weeks from now,' said Mrs Longden, 'we will celebrate a major literary anniversary with strong connections to south Cumbria. It will be two hundred years since William Wordsworth wrote one of his most famous poems. I need hardly remind *you* of the poetic legacy that Wordsworth left behind.'

'No, Mrs Longden,' said Angie. 'You need not.'

'Quite. Now then, to mark this major milestone, our school has won the chance to perform a massed reading. We will gather at Wordsworth's old school in Hawkshead to recite the "Daffodils" poem. Just imagine the scene! A hundred young voices, all chanting together, and all in perfect time.'

Angie uncrossed her legs. 'I see,' she said. 'That'll take some organizing.'

'It will, to put it mildly,' said Mrs Longden. 'And you,

Angela, are going to be the main organizer. *You* will liaise with all the pupils required and organize rehearsals. This school has been chosen as a reward for our excellent record in the arts and academia. And just so you're in no doubt as to the size of this event, it will be broadcast live on BBC Radio Four. At eleven o'clock in the morning.'

Angie felt the room, and her own head, begin to shrink. 'Is . . . is, like, anyone helping me?' she stuttered.

'You may call on other pupils,' said Mrs Longden. 'But no teachers will be involved in the preparation. And there's one other thing too. Something important.'

Angie stared at Mrs Longden in defeat. She was cornered and she knew it.

'What else, Mrs Longden?'

The headmistress held up some typed notes. 'In our briefing from the BBC, they have asked that we offer a new idea around the daffodils theme. Their broadcast will not just involve the massed reading. They want some original twist, some unusual angle on daffodils that will interest their millions of listeners. Yes, I did say millions.'

Angie edged forward. 'But . . . like what?' she almost begged. 'I don't know the first thing about daffodils.'

Mrs Longden rose from behind her huge wooden desk. 'Then you have a few hard weeks in which to learn more. And to offer up something with a special concept about daffodils. But I trust your research will not take you to Ulverston again on a school afternoon. You will have access to equipment here and use of a computer.'

Angie stood up, feeling bloodless. 'Thank you, Mrs Longden,' she said quietly.

'Make this event a success, Angela,' said the headmistress. 'The eyes and ears of Cumbria, in fact the whole country, will be upon us. Up to a hundred of our children, crammed into Wordsworth's old school to recite a wonderful poem. Two hundred years since its first known version was created. And the BBC there to learn what new and wonderful themes you have discovered about daffodils. A flower that has really become a symbol for this part of the world, thanks to Wordsworth. You may go now, Angela.'

TWELVE

The daffodils were blooming in my private little garden, hidden away behind Dad's garage and those corrugated iron sheets. They looked different every day, with a touch more yellow in the petals, or a darker orange in the trumpet.

Daffs have grown wild in this country since around 2000 BC. When starting out, you have to buy their bulbs first, then use the flowers they produce for cross-breeding. There's over eight thousand different types, but they all have a perianth (group of petals) and that inner trumpet.

After two years of growing from seed, they're like little blades of grass. I examined a small patch of my own young ones, which looked so weedy you'd think they'd never flourish. Daffs don't like getting their feet wet in winter so you need to dig deep, in well-drained soil. All this cross-breeding took time and patience. But I had plenty of time and patience, as this passion kept me well away from the estuary with its harsh memories. And with Granddad's old scutcher I could dig deep and long at my own pace.

I heard my dad knocking about in the garage behind,

and voices from the alley. Some of his Motor Heads group had come round to learn new tricks. It sounded like they were washing his prized red sports car.

'Don't rub too hard with those cloths,' Dad called. 'Clean the sides with straight strokes. Mikey, start warming that wax up. And when you begin to polish the doors . . .'

I blocked them out, working quietly so nobody heard me.

On either side of me were patches of mature daffodils. One type called King Alfred sang with yellow all over, both petals and trumpet. The other was called Girl Friend, with a white perianth and pink trumpet. They were two cross-breeds of Granddad's that I'd planted from his bulbs.

'Oi, Razzler,' shouted a mouthy lass in the alley. 'Where's your Andy, Mr Randy?'

'Haven't a clue,' said Dad, who guarded my secret life. 'Who wants him?'

'Not *me*,' gobbed the girl. 'I reckon Diana might. She been round?'

'Nope,' said Dad. 'And I ain't seen Andy since tea.'

'Oh. Tell him he's missing out. She's on his trail.'

I went almost dizzy with desire. Diana Dowder, with her ginger nut and bumpy bits, was on *my* trail. Warm quivers raided my stomach and chest. How close was I to the impossible miracle of some girl, *any* girl? I had to focus extra hard just then.

With a pair of tweezers, I pulled out the six anthers from a Girl Friend trumpet. It's done so that none of their own pollen can reach the stigma. You call this 'receiver' the Black Flower.

Using a small paintbrush, I collected King Alfred's pollen. You call this 'donor' one the Red Flower. I placed its yellow dust on Girl Friend's stigma.

Within three weeks there'd be an obvious swelling of Girl Friend's seed box. This would tell me that the pollen had been taken. First I had to place a small plastic bag around this Black Flower. It would prevent any other stray pollen reaching the stigma. It would also catch the seeds when the ovary burst.

After nature had done its stuff, I'd scatter those seeds onto a flowerbed and grow them for six years. Each seed would produce a different flower. A flower that had never before been seen on earth!

It was getting chilly when I'd finished, even with my flappy woollen hat down over my ears. There was a bit of loud fuss in the alley, so I slipped quietly through the back door and locked it. I strolled up through the garage and into the narrow lane behind Dayton Street.

Lounging against our back wall were three girls. Diana Dowder was in the middle, her short ginger hair around a chunky neck. I went closer, shyly, like I was going indoors. The two other girls melted away, knuckles in mouths to choke their giggles.

I stood before Diana as she slowly chewed gum and

eyeballed me. Her nose was like a daffodil bulb, all podgy and round. She wore dark eyeliner, a bit streaked.

She stopped chewing and stared back.

'Want a photo?' she asked, waving her mobile at me. 'Click, click,' she said, then went into silly laughs.

'If you like,' I said, smiling like a fool. 'What other pics you got on there?'

Diana went flicking through as I stood beside her. I saw images of her various Dowder clan relatives; some naked, or drunk, or snogging, or in the bath.

'Nice,' I said as a picture of Malky baring his teeth flashed up.

'Wanna go for a walk?' said Diana.

Fire raged through my stomach. 'What ... now?' I asked.

'No, dumbster. Next week.'

'Oh. OK.'

'Blimey! Course I mean *now*.'

'Oh. OK. Um, just gotta pop inside. Won't be a sec.'

'Yeah, don't be long,' said Diana. 'Give it a good shake after.'

Blushing, I fled up to my room. I glugged some of Mum's Damiana straight from the jar, fighting an urge to spit it back out. My breath stank, so I ate toothpaste from the tube and ran back downstairs.

'Hi,' I gasped, my hat's flaps flopping.

'Hi. Gonna wear that tea cosy for ever?'

I touched Mum's lovingly made headgear. 'Keeps me warm,' I mumbled.

'Something should,' Diana said, mooching along the lane. I followed like a lost dog. I didn't like to ask where we were going. I thought we might end up at Little Copse, where the younger druggies hung out. The thought of smoking that stuff made me scared, and I wanted Orange Flyer. The ground went wobbly below me.

We went on in silence, then cut through an overgrown path up towards The Slaggy. Its lunar rocks glowed with memories of the molten furnace they once sprang from. We sat on a clump of raised earth, looking out at the dark and fateful bay. I edged closer, feeling Diana's motherly hips against mine.

'What was it like?' she asked.

I looked at her bulby nose. 'What?' I said.

'You know, that time. When those two tourists copped it. What happened?'

I felt the warm flames inside me go cold. Was this all she wanted? A close-up account of the tragedy?

'Can't really remember,' I mumbled. 'Dunno. It's all misty.'

Diana gently pulled my ear, then tickled my cheek. Flames returned like an inferno.

'Well,' I began, 'I think I just froze. But it was also like I couldn't believe they would both really sink under. And then my legs wouldn't move. Not at first anyway. Not until it was too late.'

Diana nodded, her gingery hair bobbing. That herby Damiana was kicking in, yet I also felt an urge to confess. The words came bubbling out.

'But nothing could save them, not even this weird old man that I found. The sands kept up their slow ... suck-suck-sucking, and the two of them out there could see me, or see someone, and the father shouted at me like he'd shouted at his boy just earlier. And the rescue helicopter finally came, but even that was like a hopeless toy. It landed somewhere around here, near the slag banks, and at last its awful blades shut up and the air went still again.'

Diana stroked my hand, but I was off on one.

'That's all I remember really. That, and the daffodils blooming in Granddad's back garden when the police took me there. Only he wasn't at home. Mum and Dad weren't home either. Wow, I'd forgotten that. They were both out at a peace festival in Ulverston, while I was watching someone else's family get destroyed.'

I felt the tears rise, and swiped at them. Diana took off my hat and nuzzled me.

'Poor thing,' she said. 'Poor sweetie.'

At which point I acted like some demon, swept away with desire. I toppled onto Diana Dowder, forcing my minty mouth over hers. I wrestled her legs apart with mine as her tongue lashed my teeth. My jeans were bulging, and it felt like the zip would burst clean off. But this was a Dowder girl, and she shoved me away easily and roughly, then sat up gasping.

'Leave off, mate!' she said. 'Wow, it's always the quiet ones.'

'Sorry,' I muttered.

'Back off a bit, super stud,' she said. 'I'm only fifteen. I'm not a pushover.' She bit her fingers and looked over the bay to where Askam's lights were twinkling. I crawled across and touched her knee. She pulled away.

'Sorry,' I said again.

'Well . . . yeah! What good's sorry?'

We sat listening to the Irish Sea slosh about in the estuary. A gull screeched above, like it was mad at me for being so brutal. I hung my head. All was quiet, but for the birds and the bay. Barrow's distant shipyards stood like matchstick sculptures on the far shore. The mountains and moorland opposite were dark archways to heaven.

Diana finally broke into giggles. 'Are you on Viagra? Does The Razzler take it?'

'No.' I smiled. 'I just get high on nature. And on natural things.'

'Oh. You're well weird.'

We walked the long way back, going along a rough road behind the beach. Just above the sands was a large and gloomy house. It stood atop the estuary and had a commanding view of both sea and town. This was where Malky lived with various remnants of his clan. The house had large dark windows that always gave the impression of someone watching you. An old gunboat's gunsights poked out from the top storey. A small outhouse was built to one side. We saw smoke rising from its chimney, and a faint glow inside.

'What's going on in there?' I asked.

Diana shrugged. 'Malky's private business,' she said. 'No one asks. So don't you bother.'

'Why do you call him Malky?' I asked. 'Why don't you say "Dad" instead?'

Diana punched me with a tough fist. 'Oi, what is all this? You a social worker? I don't call him Dad 'cos he ain't ever acted much like a dad. It's not like I even live with him.'

'Oh,' I said. 'Sorry. My dad's not very normal either.'

'He is compared to mine. The Razzler's a flaming lollipop lady next to Malky.'

As we turned back into town, we passed the church where Mr Tyson's grave lay surrounded by my heart of Mystic daffs.

'Hey, look,' said Diana. 'There's that Angie Hutchinson. The school nerd's out late tonight.'

Angie's leggy figure was rustling in various large bags by the church door. She looked around as if afraid of being seen, her white face so haunting in the moonlight. She stuffed something into a bin liner, pulled out what looked like a short skirt, then left quickly.

'Probably nicking someone's posh underwear,' said Diana. 'She came into our detention class earlier, asking for volunteers to learn this dumb poem by William Birdsworth.'

'Um, I think it's William *Words*worth,' I said, and got another hard bang on the arm.

As we arrived back in Dayton Street, my dad came lurching along with hot food wrapped in newspaper. He saw us approach and yelled out, 'Yowzer! Anyone for a chip butty?'

Diana turned to me. 'Your turn to ask *me* out next time,' she said. Then she ran up to my dad and dug into his chips like a half-starved orphan.

THIRTEEN

On Saturday morning I opened our front door to let Dad's breakfast fumes escape. I stood in the doorway, breathing fresh spring air and charred animals. Just then, Malcolm 'Malky' Dowder came by. He wore a sleeveless black top that showed off scary tattoos on his heavy arms. On his left one was the tattooed face of London gangster, Reggie Kray. The right arm showed Ronnie Kray, his brother. These two former villains were Malky's great heroes.

Malky was pushing a pram containing his latest off-shoot. He saw me lurking and shoved the pram up to me. I looked inside. A pink monkey glared back with all of its father's hostility. A baseball bat lay beside the wild child.

I swallowed hard as Malky towered over me, one hand on our door frame. I tried not to stare at his wonky right eye. People said you could never catch Malky out, as he was always looking in two different directions.

'Now then,' he said as I quaked in his shadow. His breath stank like ancient eggs. 'Now then, I hear you've been keeping company with our Diana.'

My bladder was bursting with terror. What had Diana

said? Had she accused me of assault, or even worse?

Malky carried on without waiting for a reply. 'Thing is, lad, once you're in with us Dowders, it's for life. You understand? We look after our own, and we keep our own folks real close. So if you're planning on making Diana your little lady, just remember that we believe in loyalty. No two-timing, no running out when things get hard. You hear me, son?'

'Y-yes, Malky,' I stuttered. 'I mean, Mr Dowder.'

He grinned a golden mouth of caps and fillings. 'That's OK then. You can call for her tonight, around eight o'clock. Keep it clean.'

And away he stomped, gripping that pram with white knuckles. I shivered back inside, locking the door.

'What was that about, Andy?' Dad stood right behind me in the shadows.

'Huh?' I said, acting the innocent.

'What's all that about you and Diana Dowder?' asked Dad.

'Heck knows,' I said. 'I've been once on a walk with her. We're only fifteen. Sounds like he's getting us married off.'

Dad clasped his head. 'I *said* be careful. I *said* don't go messing.'

'I *wasn't* messing,' I lied. 'Well, not very much.'

I took a long walk later around the bay. Our estuary is not like a beach, where it's just a long strip of sand in one direction. Looking down from the air, the Millom landscape thumps outwards like a clenched fist into the bay, so the tide has to curve its way around this big chunk. The town itself lies about half a mile inland. All the narrow streets seem to lead towards the sea, with glimpses of green banks or mountains at the end of each one.

You can stand on the Bridge Road in town, gazing to the other side of the estuary. From there, you see how the land bulges out in a big blob. It's like the head of a rounded spade.

First I went over to the lagoon, which looks so calm on sunny spring days. As you come inland from the sea, there's the lighthouse and the wooden observation hut. And stretching out below the hut is the lagoon, with old mining works sunken deep down. The water is aqua blue, with no trace of the last red rocks rusting below. Since the speed restrictions came into force on Cumbria's lakes, you often get wild idiots hammering their speedboats around the lagoon.

The lagoon is the largest stretch of coastal open water in north-west England. And it's enclosed by an old sea wall, which was built to keep the water out of the mines at high tide. When the last mines were closed, the pumps were turned off and the workings got flooded. The lagoon has become a reserve for wild birds, and attracts bird-watchers from everywhere. It's surrounded by scrub and grassland, with little pathways leading into different wildlife habitats. There's rare plants and endangered bird species around the nature reserve. It's amazing how quickly nature reclaims its own when industry's day has passed by.

I went and sat on a crazy creation called The Blocks. This was also built to protect the mines, and it lies at the back of the beach nearest the lighthouse. The first sea wall erected here was a rigid structure, which cracked as the mining land subsided. Then gigantic cranes appeared many years ago and made this other landmark.

The Blocks are just what they sound like. The most enormous square chunks of concrete, all tumbled together like dice. When the tide hits these cubes, it gets broken up. They're so big that even the high water in spring is below their top level.

I felt safe sitting on them, up above the beach below. That day, the tide was out and the sand lay golden brown before me. I closed my eyes, listening to the seagulls, and basked like a seal in the warmth.

I wandered home along the beach road, with Malky's ghostly mansion in the distance. Smoke was rising again from the little outhouse beside it. A burly security guy was pacing around the front. Those old gunboat gun-sights glinted from a top window. I'm sure they swivelled for a second, and pointed right at me.

It was time to think about my date that night with Diana, arranged by Malky for eight o'clock. There was only one thing I really wanted from Diana, being honest.

But after my morning warning from Malky I wasn't even up for that any more.

'What the hell are *they*?'

I stood on Diana's council-house doorstep, a bouquet of flowers in my fist.

'Daffodils,' I said. 'They're called Golden Glories.' I offered them up.

She took the bunch, held them to her swollen nose and made a face.

'Where d'you nick these from?' she laughed.

'I didn't *nick* them. I . . . It doesn't matter.'

On a table behind the door lay some fast-food flyers and junk mail. Diana dumped the daffodils down on top of that lot.

She said, 'You should've brought some booze instead, you prawn. Hang on a sec.' She went back inside, where a reality TV show was booming out. I heard the wail of a flat singing voice, and then howls of laughter and abuse from those watching in the front room. Diana came back with a big bottle of Strongbow cider.

'OK,' she said, slamming the door. 'Let's go and get crazy.' She squeezed me between the legs, making my mouth fall open in painful shock.

FOURTEEN

We walked away from the little town, and up a grassy slope onto The Slaggy. Its crumbling white debris was like moon dust in the dusk. I stood on the edge of this raised ground, watching the last sunset embers over distant leathery hills. Diana went skidding down the bank, the Strongbow bottle held high like a weapon. And like a modern Viking maiden she went charging across the marshes, as if laying siege to unseen forces. In fact, all she did was lay waste to Granddad's tree-shape of Golden Glories. I went chasing down after her as she kicked through his blooming daffodils on the grassy ridge.

'Hey!' I shouted. 'Be careful.'

Diana turned her gormless gaze on me. 'What is it?' she said, looking at the golden-green pattern around her.

'It's a tribute,' I said. 'It's like, um, the tree of life.'

Diana tutted, and kicked out again. 'Stupid nature freaks,' she said. 'Can't they stick to their own gardens if they wanna plant stuff like this?'

We took the rocky sea road that used to be an iron-mine railway. It curves from the eastern edge of Millom, around towards the lighthouse and lagoon. Diana swigged on the cider, and I took a few little gulps to be sociable. She slagged off all her school teachers, and most of her family and mates, as I listened to the night wind rippling off the bay.

We reached the Hodbarrow lighthouse. It was built on the sea wall that became The Blocks. Now its light is powered by solar energy. I liked this big metal thing, with its red and white hoops going a bit rusty. It was like a solid symbol of protection, even if it was no longer in real use.

Diana kicked its base with what sounded like a steel toecap. 'Ugly old thing,' she said. 'They should pull it down for scrap. You want some more?' She thrust the cider bottle at me like my manhood was being challenged. I slurped the final sticky dregs. Diana tore the empty container from my hands and chucked it onto The Blocks. It bobbed on the breeze over those great concrete cubes. The sea was breaking below The Blocks in its endless, hopeless quest to wear them down.

The estuary was dark and cold. I heard a bird's tuneful song from the lagoon beyond the bird-watching hut. It might have been a willow warbler. Then came the familiar loud trumpet call of the Canada geese. I whispered, 'Wow, just listen. So wild and strange.'

Diana made a face and covered her ears. 'Bloody racket,' she said.

I wanted to go into the hut, out of the cooling night, and watch the birds. But my date had other ideas.

'Right,' said Diana, pushing up close. 'Here then.'

'Huh? I said. 'Here *what*?'

She prodded her head, as if talking to a dumb alien. 'Let's do it . . . *here*,' she said.

It was so chilly that I felt lifeless. And I hadn't taken any Damiana to get me going.

'Hang on,' I said. 'Last time out here, you said—'

'Well, last time was our first date, thicky. Now we're going steady, we can move things on.'

'Are we . . . going steady?' I mumbled. A lifetime of Millom and Malky was looming in the next few seconds.

'You bought me flowers, we've been out walking. What d'you call *that*?'

'Hmm. Good point. Only, the thing is, I'm a bit busy right now. Lots of school work on . . . My granddad's not very well either. I think it's all the old mining dust in his lungs. He's in this care home out in Ulverston, and he might not—'

'Oh, flaming forget it! You great big . . . big-eared wuss!' She stamped away back onto the old road above the shadowy beach.

'Diana?' I called. 'Hang on. All I meant was . . .'

She turned and gave me two fingers, then ran. Diana moved fast for a big girl. Her cosy rump vanished into the night. I gave chase, suddenly worried that she might go to Malky and get him to rough up my dad. She headed towards The Slaggy, its rocks glowing like cold coals. I caught up with her on the marshes below Granddad's daffodil tree-shape.

'I'm sorry,' I panted. 'It's just that—'

She kicked me on the knee with a steely boot, then bombed off again. I shouted with pain, feeling my bones wail.

I heard someone cough behind me. A girl sat alone, up on the grassy bank where Granddad's daffs were glowing. It was Angie Hutchinson, her hair flowing, dressed in a woolly shawl and tartan skirt. No DJ Terry for company tonight.

I had to find my dad and warn him about Diana before our house was burned down. But I caved in to beauty and joined Angie there for a moment. She sounded a bit sad.

'Hey, you,' she said. 'You got girlfriend trouble?'

'*No*,' I protested. 'She's not my—'

'Who d'you think created something so beautiful?' asked Angie. She brushed her fingers through the petals of those Golden Glories, like a mermaid trailing her hand in the sea. 'I mean,' she said, 'some great landscape artist must have planted these like this. But for who? For what?'

I couldn't resist telling her. 'Actually, it was my granddad. He planted them after something bad happened once.'

Angie sat up. 'Oh. Oh yeah, sorry. You're the boy who saw that . . . thing happen once. Out on the estuary.'

'Yeah. That's me.'

'Right. But what a beautiful tribute. I should write a poem about this.'

'Yeah?' I said. 'Granddad would like that. He loves poetry.'

Angie looked closely at me. 'He does? Listen, tell me more about your granddad and these daffodils. It might be important.'

I felt my toes curl with desire, but gave in to family duty. 'Listen,' I said, 'I'd really love to stay. But there's someone I've got to find.'

'OK,' said Angie. 'You go find them. I'll stay and talk to these amazing flowers. But I wanna know more about your granddad. He could really help me . . .'

I gave her a shy wave, then tore into Millom, high on Angie's beautiful words. I found my dad in the chippy, swaying after a night on the beer.

'Dad, listen!'

'Andy! Wassup, geezer?'

'I think I've upset Diana Dowder. Malky's lot might be calling round.'

'Oh heck, mate. What you done now?'

'Nothing. She just went weird on me.'

'Be all right,' Dad said. 'Me and Malky get along fine. I'll sort it.'

He ordered a veggie burger for me, and fried fish for himself.

'There you go, Randy,' said the chip maestro. 'The last bit of haddock for tonight.'

'Cheers, pal,' said Dad. He picked up his hot parcel from the counter. Then someone tapped him firmly on the back. We looked round at a bulky, broken-nosed bloke. He was older than Dad, but twice the weight.

'I'll fight you for it,' he said.

'*What?*' went Dad.

'I said, I'll fight you for it. That last piece of haddock.'

'You're joking,' Dad laughed.

'No.'

'Look, mate. I'm not into fighting. I got here first, and I'm taking this fish.'

The big bloke didn't sound angry. 'I know you got here first,' he said. 'That's why I'm offering to fight you for it. Fair's fair.'

'Oh, just take it!' shouted Dad, shoving the bundle across. 'You sad sap. Come on, Andy.'

'Cheers, mate. Hey, are you that Randy Kindness?'

'*Yeah*. What of it?'

'I'm Malky Dowder's cousin. They call me Vinnie. I'll tell him how generous you were. G'night.'

We walked home stuffing my chips and veggie burger down, laughing and swaying.

'It's like Granddad always says.' I smiled. 'They should skim off the scum in this town, and leave the decent nuggets like us.'

'A good bloke, your granddad,' said Razzle. 'He any better yet?'

'I'll go over next weekend and see. Got loads of school work to do tomorrow.'

We sat up late, playing mellow Neil Young albums. He sang about a girl wearing something pretty and white, and how they'd both go dancing that night. I thought of Angie Hutchinson, and her poetic praise for those Golden Glories.

'Dad,' I said, 'what causes that funny feeling you get? The one when you see a girl, and it's like something's itching in your guts.'

Dad leaned forward, a cigar in one hand. 'That, my son . . . *that* is the next generation pressing into being. It's all the little genes inside you saying to the girl, *I wanna mate with you. I want to give you babies*. It's purely natural.'

'Right,' I said. 'I see.'

'Is that how Diana Dowder makes you feel?'

'No,' I sighed, aware of a new and deep sadness. 'But Angie Hutchinson makes me go gooey like that.'

'Oh, Angie. Hmm. Not sure who I'd fear most for a married relation. Malky, or Ma Hutchinson. At least with Malky you'd get a decent wedding reception.'

Dad hit the brandy and started burbling. 'The mad rush of young love,' he said. 'I remember it well. When it's all new and bruised and sexy and beautiful. Then those first few steps are washed away in the ocean of life . . .'

He was getting all maudlin. He started to sniffle, and I knew he was thinking about Mum and all the mistakes he'd made. I patted his mohican hair and left him to it.

FIFTEEN

Millom was in deep shock one morning. A car carrying two teenage boys had crashed on the road out of nearby Haverigg. The accident happened in the early hours, and one of the lads was dead. They'd been to visit a friend in Haverigg prison.

Haverigg lies right on the coast nearby, and the prison sits behind security fencing. From the outside it looks like a load of small factory units. Wind turbines rise from the flat fields on either side.

At the end of the prison's visiting hours, the two lads had hit some local pubs. Later, they'd driven off up the coast in search of nightlife, but only made it to Silecroft beach. Realizing there wasn't any action, they'd sped back down towards Millom to pick up the main route back home to Barrow.

Some time around one a.m., the driver took a sharp corner at speed. Going down the road to school later that morning, we all saw loads of police tape. The red-brick wall of an old factory was dented and charred. The sloping verge of grass across from it was gouged with tyre marks.

The death of anyone, young or old, always hit me

hard after the events of six years before. And I knew what had to be done that night.

Remember I told you about Red and Black Flowers? They're the ones that give and receive pollen when you're cross-breeding. Back home that evening, I checked the Girl Friend daffs that I'd bred with some King Alfreds. Sure enough, inside the plastic bag I'd wrapped the Girl Friend in, the seed box had burst. Lots of tiny grains were speckled about inside.

To me, these seeds were like magic gold dust. I could sprinkle them anywhere, knowing the full glory they'd finally display.

I waited until after dark, then skated over to that grimy old factory near the school. The police tape fluttered softly in the wind. A few bunches of flowers wrapped in cellophane were already piling up nearby. Someone had written a card that said, *Will so miss u*.

Working quickly, glancing around, I burrowed deep into the nearby embankment with my scutcher. It really was so much quicker and easier than using a trowel or small spade. In went the seeds, placed a few centimetres apart. I could've used existing bulbs that would appear next spring. But this new breed was one of my own creations, and anything planted from seed takes six years to grow. In my heart I had already named this new species 'Angie'.

I didn't plant the seeds in any particular shape. But I made sure that enough went in to cover this bed of tragic earth in beauty. I had no idea then how the final flower would look; what colour its petals, what size and shade its trumpet.

I tipped my head back and watched a shooting star plunge through the night sky, like a golden raindrop down a dark window. Then I bagged the scutcher and hopped onto Orange Flyer. But instead of going straight home, I rode over to the churchyard where Mr Tyson lay buried. I wanted to see how well my heart of daffodils gleamed by his grave, under the half-moon.

Mr Tyson's resting place was now easy to find, even at night. You got hit by a heady scent from five metres off. It made you feel giddy and loved-up. I could sniff daffodils for fun, like some kids got high on glue.

The Mystic daffs were awash with sunshine and scarlet. No heart had ever shone at night with such brilliance. In the shadows, the petals were almost a dark shade of gold. And each trumpet was rimmed with red, like a huge kiss.

Mrs Tyson had left a card propped at the base of this heart. It read, *Thank you, God, for such mercy.*

I smiled, and grabbed Orange Flyer. But up ahead by the church, beyond the sea of gravestones, a figure was rooting around in some black sacks. I heard the rustle of bin liners. Then my nose twitched with pollen and I sneezed. The figure leaped up sharply and stood watching me. It turned and ran, though even in the gloom I recognized Angie Hutchinson's flowing locks and long limbs. Her hair was a red-yellow blend, like those Mystic daffs behind me.

I went up to the church door, where a number of bags and sacks were stashed. A notice on the door said, JUMBLE SALE COLLECTION POINT. Several looked as though they'd been torn open. Angie was nowhere in sight.

I hopped onto the Flyer and hit the pavement. Just near the humpy bridge through town was the Bridge Café. It had a nicely landscaped garden and poultry pens down below. I heard something squawk and wondered if a fox had got in among the livestock. I stood on my skateboard and peeped over the brick bridge.

Down in the garden, streaked with moonlight, were Diana Dowder and Jason Brindley. Jase was the Bronx Crewer who sometimes mocked me about what happened when I was nine. He wore a black and white tracksuit thing, and the usual baseball cap. It was hard to tell what Diana was wearing, as Jase had her trapped in front of him by the far wall. Both were grinding and groaning. And I felt not a hint of hurt or anything. In fact, I laughed loud enough for Jase to twist his spotty face round, but I ducked from sight. I skated home, whistling, and trying to squash my FA Cup ears.

Malcolm Dowder called by on Saturday morning. I was helping Dad wash the front door. The Razzler had been out the previous night, and spilled his chips 'n' mushy peas everywhere while fumbling for the house key.

Malky lurched down Dayton Street like a gunfighter heading for the saloon. His wonky eye glared at me, his good one fixed on Dad.

'I hear you looked after my cousin Vinnie t'other night,' he said.

'What?' said Dad. 'Oh, the haddock thing. Well, he seemed pretty hungry.'

'Very generous,' said Malky. 'Take care of our own, don't we?'

He gave me a short nod. Clearly he didn't know Diana had found fresh bait in Jason Brindley. Malky lifted his sheepskin coat, looked around, then slid something out. Something silvery.

It was a gun. A piece. A revolver. A shooter. Call it what you like, but it was the first one I'd ever seen up close. Malky held it like a kid's toy, twirling it around his finger.

'Between the both of us, Randolph,' said Malky quietly to Dad, 'things might turn a little rough around here soon. And as you're nearly family, I'm gonna offer you this little beauty. Not for keeps, but strictly on a hire basis. Say, fifty quid a week?'

Dad stared through his tinted shades at Malky. 'You're kidding,' he said. 'In Millom? I know it's not perfect, but surely . . . ?'

Malky shook his head. 'You never know what might be around the corner.'

'Right,' said Dad. 'Er, well I think we're OK

actually. But if we need anything, I'll give you a call.'

Malky shoved the gun back under his tan coat. 'You do that, Randolph,' he said. 'You'll know where to find me.' He stalked off down the street, kicking a black cat that dared to cross his path. We both stared after him.

'What's he mean, *turn rough*?' I asked.

'Heck knows,' Dad said. 'Didn't like to ask.'

'What's his business, anyway?' I said. 'He never works for anyone, always has loads of cash, and I keep seeing smoke rising from a building near his house.'

Dad leaned back on our washed door. 'Drugs in the main,' he said. 'Those little caravans you sometimes see around this area are used as stash sites. People turn up to score but have no money, so they offer jewellery stolen from their own families, or from anywhere. It pays well, whatever he does. I heard he bought a local house last week for eighty-five grand. Malky just turned up with the cash in a suitcase and handed it over.'

'Strewth,' I said. 'I'm glad that Diana's found someone else.'

Dad laughed. 'Oh, help,' he said. 'Here comes another local legend.'

It was Mrs Hutchinson, in a granny shawl and brown tights. How did such an old dowdy produce a poetic beauty like Angie?

'Good morning, Mr Kindness!' She beamed. 'I wonder if you have any cosy community news for me today?'

Dad stroked his chin. 'Nothing much, ma'am,' he

said. 'Nothing really new to report. But Mr Dowder was here a moment ago. He just told me some interesting local news.'

Mrs Hutchinson looked doubtful, and peered at Dad over her metal specs. 'Are you quite sure, Mr Kindness?' she asked.

Dad put a hand over his heart. 'Call me Randy,' he said. 'And Mr Dowder has a finger on the town's pulse like no one else. Honest.'

Without reply, Mrs Hutchinson turned back into the street. Malky was heading for the bookie's as Ma Hutch clip-clopped after him in wooden clogs. 'Mr Dowder!' she called. 'One moment please! Mr Dowder . . .'

Dad rubbed his hands with joy. 'Right!' he said. 'I think a lunchtime pint is in order. Give my love to your mum, if she can still bear to think of me. I'm at the doctor's first thing on Monday, if I don't see you before then. Have a nice weekend.'

Sixteen

The next bus out of Millom to Ulverston had only one other passenger. Angie Hutchinson. She sat on the right, by a window, buried in some intellectual journal. I sat on the left side, right across from her. Angie wore her round specs, and the kind of uncool gear most girls wouldn't leave their bedrooms in. Her clothes must be of her mother's choosing. A green cardigan, flowery long-sleeved shirt and brown corduroy trousers. She also had the sort of boring black shoes that nurses wear.

Angie gave no sign that she'd noticed me, but as the bus pulled away I glanced across. She was peeking at me from behind the pages. I smiled, but she stuffed her face back into her reading. The paper's cover said, *The London Literary Review*. It bore the names of several top writers, some sounding foreign. Angie's hands were gripping the paper oddly, crushing the sides, like she had something else hidden in there.

My eyeballs began to hurt with all the sly glimpses I gave Angie. It's not easy keeping your face straight ahead, and your eyes sneaking sideways.

Suddenly the bus driver slammed on the brakes. I was thrown forward onto the seat in front. I got a flash of some dog tearing across the road. Angie was flung towards me, her *London Literary Review* flapping into the aisle. Another magazine flew out of the *Literary Review*, like a freed bird. I sat back with a jolt, and it landed in my lap.

It was *Kerrang!*, the weekly rock mag that I always bought every Friday.

The driver swore and smacked the window. The dog fled into nearby farm fields as me and Angie looked at each other.

'You two OK?' shouted the driver.

'Yeah.'

'Fine.'

'Sorry about that,' he said. 'The little sod came from nowhere.' He pulled away again very slowly, as if an army of suicidal hounds was waiting in the hedges.

I handed *Kerrang!* back to Angie. From somewhere I found a voice to address her.

'Good feature about a new band on page nine,' I said. I leaned closer, as if we had revealed ourselves as members of the same cult. 'My dad says they're gonna be the next Hawkwind.'

Angie adjusted her glasses, which had slipped during the doggy drama. Her luscious hair was tied back in a ponytail. She'd gone rather red.

'The next who?' she said.

'Hawkwind,' I said. 'Kinda trippy, heavy, psychedelic stuff. Y'know? Made stacks of records.'

Angie nodded. 'Right,' she said. 'Thanks for the tip.' Her cheeks blushed like beetroots as she folded up the two journals. For the rest of the journey she stared out at the passing landscape and the small sleepy villages.

As we got off, I nervously asked, 'You meeting someone?'

She nudged her glasses. 'A bit of library research,' she said. 'Into daffodils.'

Angie watched me closely, looking for a response. I felt my ears blazing.

'Oh, y-yeah,' I gulped. 'Mrs Longden said in assembly that you're putting together that Wordsworth event in Hawkshead. Well, you can sign me up.'

'I *can*?' Angie looked thrilled.

'Yeah. To be one of the Daffodil poem readers. Be nice to get shut of Millom for a morning.'

'Uh-huh. Anything else you can offer me? About daffodils, I mean.'

'Don't think so,' I said, swallowing a large lump.

Angie smiled like a sneaky cat. 'OK,' she said, walking off. 'We'll soon see what you really know, Mr Flower Power.'

I hardly recognized my granddad that day. When I went into his upstairs room in the care home, the sunlight washed everything in a holy glow. It bathed the bed where he lay, looking so much weaker than last time. His face was no longer ruddy from endless hours out in a garden in all weathers. It seemed shrunken, ashy, and maybe for the first time ever he hadn't shaved. His white hair was thin and flat. Without his glasses on, I'm not sure he could even see me properly.

I crept in and whispered, 'Granddad? Are you awake?'

He stirred slightly, propped up against pale pillows. His voice was weak. 'Andrew?'

'Yes, I'm here,' I said quietly, edging onto a bedside chair.

'Now then, lad,' croaked Granddad. 'What news?'

I had some photos on my mobile of the daffodil heart I'd done for Mr Tyson.

'Look,' I said. 'Look how your Mystics came out after I planted them last year.'

I flicked through the images, holding them close to Granddad's face. He breathed slowly and roughly, his eyes trying to focus.

At last he whispered, 'Always had such large petals, those Mystics.'

'That's right,' I said. 'And I've also cross-bred two of your own species. The King Alfred and the Girl Friend.'

Granddad sighed, his throat rattling. 'And what might you call this new flower, if it succeeds?'

'Angie,' I said. 'She's a girl in Millom. She's so pretty and clever. And we like the same music, which is dead important. Like me, she seems to have a secret life, though I'm not sure it's one you'd approve of.'

Granddad tried to smile. 'We all have secrets,' he said, his voice breaking. 'A secret someone. Or a secret sorrow.'

I put my mobile on the bed, staring at one of my flowery photos, and listened to chirpy birds in the trees outside. The care home's lawn had just been cut, giving off a summery warmth of grassy freshness.

'I've been using your scutcher,' I said. 'It really burrows deep into the earth. Just like you said.'

Granddad nodded vaguely and stared at the bedroom door ahead of him. His eyes went misty and moist. I had to lean closer to hear him. 'There's something I must tell you,' he said. 'Before it's too late. And then you can decide whether to forgive me or not. I'll understand if you can't.'

He shifted about in the bed, frowning with some hidden pain.

I said, 'There's nothing I wouldn't forgive you, Granddad. What on earth is it?'

His eyes flickered and looked at the bedside cabinet. 'In there,' he said. 'No, not up there . . . right down at the bottom. There's a folder with some photographs.'

I rooted around among Granddad's personal stuff, his dry shaving brush and spare glasses. Hidden at the back was a leather folder, A4 sized, packed with loose photographs. I pulled it out and handed it across.

Some of the photos were in colour, and I recognized many of Granddad with Grandma before she died. I was only five when she passed away, and I could just about remember a kindly lady who always had a bag of sweets for me. Granddad shuffled the pictures, then laid one of them out on his bedding.

It showed Granddad from years ago, with a full head of grey-brown hair. He still had the same blackly rimmed glasses, but his face was younger and softer. Grandma stood on his left, with curly grey hair and square glasses. But an attractive and mature lady stood to Granddad's right. She wore a dark dress, necklace and silk scarf. She looked like a vintage Hollywood actress from the silent movie era.

Granddad said, 'The other lady is Mrs Moorhouse. Irene Moorhouse. She was the wife of my best friend, Peter Moorhouse. He worked in the mines right beside me, and we shared an allotment too. We were all very good friends, and Irene often came to church with me on Sunday evenings. Peter never came to church, so Irene liked someone to go with.'

'That's nice,' I said. 'But didn't Grandma mind that?'

Granddad closed his eyes. Both lids trembled with the effort of blocking tears. 'I think she *did* mind,' he said. 'Whenever Irene arrived, she'd say, "Oh, here's your girl-friend turned up again." Sometimes your grandma came with us, just to keep an eye on me.'

I looked again at the photo before me. It was taken on Silecroft beach, up the coast from Millom. I recognized the stony car park behind the sands.

'Peter passed away four years after your grandma

died. I looked after Irene in the way that she cared for me when your grandma went. But then one Sunday she phoned up to say she must see me. It sounded urgent, so I hurried around the bay to Askam, where she and Peter had retired to. When I got there, she made a confession of her feelings for me. She said that now we were both widowers, we could be together like she had always wanted.'

I felt my granddad's cold hand. 'That wasn't a sin, Granddad,' I said. 'What did you tell her?'

Granddad lay back, looking shattered. 'I said I had promised your grandma I would never marry again. And I told your grandma that, the night before she died. I could never have broken my promise, but Irene got very upset when I told her this. She was lonely and full of grief, and I didn't feel safe leaving her alone just then.'

I pressed Granddad's hand again. 'You did right,' I said. 'But why do you have to tell me all this?'

Granddad sighed from a scratchy throat. 'Because it's what was happening elsewhere that still haunts me. It was the same Sunday afternoon when you saw that tragic drowning on the bay. That very same Sunday. And I was supposed to be looking after you. Your parents were at a peace festival, and I left you alone and uncared for. When you needed me the most, I failed you. And I am so sorry I wasn't there that day.'

I shivered, despite the glaring sunshine. 'I understand,' I said. 'But is Irene still alive?'

Granddad was dozing now, his breaths growing deeper. 'Yes,' he said. 'But to ease my guilt at leaving you alone that day, I never went to see her again. I always had deep feelings for Irene too, but I could never betray your grandma. Not even when she went from this life. Maybe I'll soon be with her again. When I go from all this sunshine, into the sunless land. That's how Wordsworth put it.'

'You'll get better soon,' I urged. 'And there's nothing to forgive. You did what was right.'

But my granddad was asleep seconds later, breathing like someone with a terrible load on his chest. Or an eternal weight in his heart.

SEVENTEEN

I skated down into Ulverston, deep in quiet thought. Two phrases were tumbling through my mind as Orange Flyer's wheels rumbled below me.

We all have secrets, said Granddad. *A secret someone. Or a secret sorrow.*

I must see Granddad again very soon, and tell him not to worry about that fateful Sunday afternoon.

We'll soon see what you really know, said Angie. *Mr Flower Power.*

This was more worrying. If Angie thought she was on to my secret life, there must be a reason. What clues had I given her? I'd let slip about my granddad's interest in daffodils, the night I saw Angie alone up on The Slaggy. And the other night I'd been admiring my flowery heart-shape in the graveyard while she was acting strangely near the church door. Maybe she was just guessing, and trying to tease some confession out of me to help with her Wordsworth poetry event for the BBC.

I was glad to reach Ulverston's small town centre and find it full of life and colour. It was Buddhist Festival week. The cobbled streets were packed with people in purple robes and yellow garments. Some were walking barefoot, some carrying walking staffs. All were shaven headed, so you couldn't always tell the men from the women. A small group was singing and chanting by the war memorial, tapping drums or tambourines.

There's this monastery about two miles from town, on the coast road. It's called Conishead Priory, and some Buddhists run it as a kind of retreat from reality. You can go there to rest up, work the gardens, cook, clean or whatever. In return, you get to stay in this tranquil haven, and meditate the day away with like minds. Once a year they have a big festival, and the town gets overrun by monkish types in their wine-coloured gowns.

They always buy stuff in the wholefood shop where Mum works. I went in, tucking Orange Flyer under my arm. You could hardly move for all the smiley saints with stubbly scalps. They greeted and blessed and hugged. I edged around them and browsed among the 'male self-help' section. I recognized Damiana, and saw various bottles of stuff called things like Saw Palmetto, Ginseng and Gingko Biloba.

After a shy glance around, I picked up a white plastic jar. It was labelled HORNY GOAT WEED. Even I could work out what this was for. A smug smiley couple were pictured on the front, looking more like they were about to hit Sainsbury's than slip among the sexy sheets.

'Hello, Andrew,' said one of the shop helpers. I dropped the bottle in shock and shoved it on a low shelf.

'Hello, Abayakurti,' I said. The guy's real name was

Paul Pickles, and he came from Kirkby Lonsdale. He used to install cables for British Telecom, have long hair and drive a Porsche to fancy restaurants. Then he took Buddhist orders, turned veggie, shaved his head and became Abayakurti. (You say it A-*bye*-a-curty.)

'Looking for anything?' He smiled and glanced down at the Horny Goat Weed jar.

'Just my mum,' I said. 'Is she about?'

'She left a message to say don't expect her home before six. She and Melissa are doing some catering up at Conishead Priory. I think she's taking you over there tomorrow.'

'Oh. Brill. Thanks, Abayakurti.'

'You're welcome, Andrew. A blessing be upon you.' He bowed slightly, then picked up the Horny Goat Weed bottle. He placed it back on a higher shelf, with another little smile.

Mum's higgledy house had some new brochures about that Skyros place. She'd also been doing research on the Internet, as there were pages of printouts on the kitchen table. I read one aloud, testing the strange place names in my mouth.

'*Part of the . . . Sporades . . . in the northern . . . Aegean . . . Skyros Island is an enchanting place. Sung about by Homer, and full of ancient memories, the island is renowned for its unique pottery, ponies, large pine forests, beautiful bays and beaches. The local community, and its age-old traditions, are still intact and thriving. The island remains one of Greece's best-kept secrets.'*

I nosed around the front room on Mum's desk, and found her passport. The date stamp and photo were new. It looked like she was off on holiday before long. I also found some documents about the house, and a load of bank statements, but this was getting snoopy. And fearing that supper might be a touch too wholesome, I set about making it myself.

'Looks good,' said Mum as we sat down later. I'd raided her recipe books to find something I could rustle up. So we tucked into Shepherdess Pie, which was mashed spuds piled onto tinned tomatoes and cooked veg. The whole thing was baked in the oven with plenty of organic cheese on top.

'How's your dad?' asked Mum.

'The usual,' I said. 'He mentioned something about seeing the doctor on Monday.'

'Good grief!' Mum said. 'He must be at death's door. Last time he went there was when I had *you* inside me. And that was only to find out how much sex we could safely have.'

'*Mum!*' I protested. 'For pity's sake!'

'Sorry. And how's your granddad doing? He was poorly last night when I went up.'

'Breathing badly,' I said. 'But he'll pull round.'

Mum stopped eating, and laid a hand on mine. 'Andy,' she said, 'you must prepare yourself for your granddad not getting better. Most likely he'll be getting worse, and quite quickly.'

I also stopped chewing. 'He's not . . . dying?' I said.

'I'm afraid he probably is. Try and see him as much as you can manage. You may not have the chance for much longer.'

The next morning was a sweet and sky-blue Sunday. It was hard to imagine my granddad lying so weakly in the care home when the sun shone like a golden daffodil. Mum drove me and her up to Conishead Priory, where she was attending a lecture on Zen meditation. The colourful and flowery Buddhists milled about, munching veggie samosas or drinking plastic beakers of fruit juice. Abayakurti was there too, dressed in his robes and sandals. He sidled up to me

'Andrew . . .' he muttered. 'About that little bottle you dropped yesterday . . .'

'Um, what bottle?' I said, feeling my face tingle.

Abayakurti mouthed, '*Horny . . . Goat . . . Weed.*' He smiled like a divine sex therapist.

'I don't remember,' I lied, wishing Mum would appear.

Abayakurti leaned closer and whispered in my ear. 'It's for older men, by and large,' he hissed. 'But if you're having problems down there, which a young boy really *shouldn't* have, come and see me. I'll fix you a herbal blend. OK?'

'Um, OK,' I said doubtfully.

'A blessing be upon you, Andrew.'

Then he was away into the bobbing and bowing throng. Chants and incense filled the bright spring morning. I wandered down to the rocky beach at the edge of the gardens and forests beyond Conishead Priory.

I held Orange Flyer closely, but still didn't dare go onto the sand. I hung about on the pebbles behind, near the tree cover, like some shy kid at a party. A line of small boulders guarded the beach as if it was private land.

Nothing had tempted me to set foot on any shoreline in the previous six years, since the bay tragedy. Sitting on The Blocks at Millom was OK, safely out of the beach's grasp. And being in sight of the sands there had grown easier with time. But to actually stand, in cold blood, directly on any sand had been impossible. The image of that father and son slowly sinking would never leave me. Their faces raised to the bleak sky for a final breath . . .

But maybe it was time for a fresh start with myself. A new life in this new season of the year.

I prowled around the stones and debris at the back of the beach. I stared at the smooth, golden-brown stretch before me. The sea around Morecambe Bay was hazy. Somewhere out there, I might spot a car ferry going across to the Isle of Man from Heysham Port.

I sat on a big rock where the beach began, with a shady forest right behind. Getting this far was easy enough, with the laces of my trainers dangling onto the sand. But to walk in a steady line towards the sea, without trembling or screaming, was a very different ambition. I sat there looking at the shore, as it slowly baked under a mustard-yellow sun. Gritty grey stones were scattered like seeds on a golden pie crust.

I grew annoyed with my own silly weakness, to see all this beauty inviting me in. I slipped off the boulder and felt warm sand beneath me. The sudden shock of it was like standing on hot coals. I took a few stumbling steps forward. The heat under my shoes grew more intense as my heart raced. But almost before I realized, I was back where I had started a moment ago. I stood between two sharp rocks, biting nervous fingers, kicking the rocks around me.

Then I suddenly sprang forward. It was like I'd been lifted by some almighty hand. The sandy ground was firm and warm again. My whole body tensed, but I made myself stand still. I looked around like a lost swimmer craving a lifebelt. And there was Orange Flyer, stashed by some rocks a few metres away.

I turned and faced my skateboard. Then I walked slowly backwards, very slowly, as far as I dared. My eyes never left the Flyer for a second. I inched further away from it, feeling feathers and driftwood crunch under my tread. My legs were numb, and sweaty drops were lining my nose. I tried closing my eyes, but felt an awful panic that someone would steal my skateboard, my lifeline above the earth.

I kept edging back with doddery steps ... until I seized up in sudden terror. My right foot was sinking. It slopped into a tide pool, crawling with crabs.

I screamed and flapped, although my foot was only ankle deep. I gurgled like a baby, trying to raise enough breath to scream. Some sense of reason returned, and I tugged my shoe out easily. I ran back up the beach, feeling it dissolve into a hundred whirlpools below me. I flung myself down by the rocks and huddled up against Orange Flyer.

It was only then that I became aware of other voices. Shouting voices, laughing voices. A pack of local kids were messing about near the tide line. They threw handfuls of sand and kicked the surf, shoving and shouting at each other. I shrank against the brown rocks and let my tired tears fall. I had failed my test before I even got started. Still scared of my own sorry shadow on a shoreline.

But the gang out there had no fear of anything. I envied them their easy fun. I watched them start a game of some sort, and wished I could be out there among them.

One of the group scrabbled around for things in the sand. Another one, in the routine white tracksuit, stood a short way off. He wielded a baseball bat, like a player waiting for the pitcher to throw. Then his mate lobbed something up to him. I thought at first it was a strange ball. It spun against the blue sky like a red star. That's when I realized what it was. Not a ball, but a live crab. The one in the tracksuit cracked it away with his baseball bat. This raised a huge cheer, mainly from the girls, who whooped it up among the seaweed strands.

After the second sickening crack of crab on wood, I skated away back up to the priory. Mum was sipping green tea on the lawn, listening to some Buddhist describe his journey through Tibet. I sat down beside her and laid my head on her broadly plump shoulder.

'Tell me about Skyros,' I whispered.

She stroked my damp hair. 'Sshh,' she said. 'That can all wait for now.'

Back home in Millom, I found Dad reading at the messy kitchen table. He had a bottle of vodka, and the remains of a Somerfield pizza beside it. I dumped down a bag of organic veg that Mum had given me.

I sat beside The Razzler. 'What you doing?' I asked.

He sighed heavily. 'There's all these new EU rules coming in for window cleaners. We've got to have portable ladders that are checked by expert people, and be aware of new height regulations.'

'Who does the checking?' I asked.

'I've got a meeting with some geezer soon. He's called – get this – the Head of Falls from a Height Team Manager. I kid you not. And I can only use a ladder from now on if there's *no*, quote, *no practical alternative!*'

I looked at the diagrams showing poles with long

extensions and water-fed poles for cleaning windows.

I read out, '*You must agitate the dirt down the window then rinse. But a water-fed pole will not remove impacted soilage.*'

I looked at Dad. 'What's . . . impacted soilage?' I asked.

Dad took the page from me and frowned over it for a minute.

'Bird shit,' he said finally. 'I think it must mean bird shit.'

He poured another large vodka and sat back. 'Heck, Andy, soon there'll be self-cleaning windows on the way. And then what's gonna happen to your poor old man?'

We sat and joked and played some blues music. Dad teased me for going off with Mum to the Buddhist house. He waved his hands, chanting, 'Ohhhmmm Navaaaahhh Shivvvaahhh!'

'I thought *you* were a hippy once,' I said.

'Oi, matey, I was always a rocker. Your mum was more the trippy type. OK, one more vodka for me, then bed. I'm at the health centre first thing.'

'What *you* off to the doctor for?' I said. 'You never go there, in case they rip into your bad eating and drinking habits.'

'Just the test results back on something. Nowt to worry over. Never had a day's illness in my life.'

* * *

It might seem to you that I lived a fairly crackers life, what with daffodils, The Razzler, mad Millom and everything. And yet that Sunday evening at home with Dad was what passed for quite normal in my world.

But it was the last normal night I would know for some time.

EIGHTEEN

The day after my trip to Conishead Priory, I went into the school library. If I'd had a dumb desire for Angie Hutchinson before the weekend, the memory of her *Kerrang!* flying into my lap had sealed it into an obsession. Amazing how finding out a girl digs the same music as you can turn her from a goodie into a goddess.

It was after lunch, and I'd eaten potato salad with hummus, followed by apple crumble. Full of lust and vitamins, I entered the new Learning Zone with its racks of books and magazines. Around the room's edge were computer stations.

The library was quiet, as the sunshine was on full spring throttle that day. Only the bookish loners, and tragic odd-balls like me, were hanging around inside. There was a big A3 sheet pinned up by the entrance. It said:

VOLUNTEERS WANTED, TO TAKE PART IN
A MAJOR BBC BROADCAST.
A HUNDRED STUDENTS NEEDED FOR RECITAL OF
WORDSWORTH'S 'DAFFODILS' POEM, IN HAWKSHEAD.
SEE ANGELA HUTCHINSON, LOWER SIXTH.
ANY WEIRD DAFFODIL INFO MUCH APPRECIATED!

There were no pupils' names entered below this. Not a single one. I put mine – *Andrew Kindness, Year 11* – in the blank space. Going round a bookcase, I saw Angie hunched at a PC in the corner. Her lovely head was held in her precious white hands. I edged closer, drawn by the daffodil image on her screen. She was scrolling up, then scrolling down, but the info was just the basic boring stuff.

She clicked onto another daffodil page, and I recognized a variety known as the Lent Lily, which you see dotted around Cumbria. I crept closer for a better look, and before I knew it I was almost behind Angie.

She swivelled in her creaky chair. Her eyes went big behind her smart specs.

'Hello there,' she said softly. 'Come to steal my copy of *Kerrang!*?'

'Got my own, thanks,' I said, staring like a loon at her fresh face. She had quite high cheekbones, a tickle of blonde hair above her lips, and even sitting down she made me feel small. Her stripy blue-black blazer got you thinking of old movies, where public schoolgirls played hockey and spoke like royalty.

'Were you lurking behind me for a reason?' she asked. 'Or d'you just like lurking? For example, let's see, around Millom churchyards at night?'

'Yeah. Do you? That's twice I've seen you up there now.' My heartbeat hit a speedy stride. Here was I, simple Andrew Kindness, having cheeky banter with the great Angie Hutch.

'Is that right?' she said. 'Perhaps you were just admiring the heart of daffodils that someone obviously planted? A very clever someone.'

'Exactly,' I said. 'I like daffodils. My granddad cross-breeds them, and he showed me some of his methods.' It was spoken aloud before I knew it, and I shut up.

But Angie sat even straighter, and fixed me with a bright smile. *'Really?* Listen, would you or your granddad—?'

'I've gotta go,' I said quickly. 'And my granddad's very ill. I've signed up for your poetry thing. Bye.'

Angie stood up. 'Hey, wait,' she said. 'Don't run off. I'd like to—'

But I was out of there sharply. I'd let enough of my secret life slip out.

The next big incident concerned our kitchen fridge at home. For years it had stood, large and white, opposite our scummy sink. Its door was draped with little magnets holding torn-out pictures of scanty models. Dad even scratched *The Razzler Rocks* onto it once, with a car key, after getting tanked up.

The rubber rim around the door's inside was crammed with crumbs. The egg tray was yellow and stained. The drinks rack held bottles of sherry, lager, gin and white wine. A crusted ketchup bottle lay on its side, lid open and leaking. The fridge light flickered like a disco strobe. Various jars and containers lurked near the back, like foodie hoodies under a dodgy streetlamp.

As for the freezer compartment, it hung with spiked stalactites. Garlic bread slices would fester there from time to time, with a 'use by' date from months before. The only greenery to crash the grubby party was the organic veg Mum gave me after my weekly visits. I always placed it in the cooler box at the bottom, edging out Dad's unwrapped cheese and wrinkled lemon wedges for his gin and tonics.

I survived on a good healthy school meal each day, and by spending my child allowance (which Dad always handed over) on half-decent grub. I liked a slimy slap-up now and then as much as anyone. But with my dad, this diet of junk he followed was almost an act of duty. It was either to punish himself for losing Mum, or to get back at her somehow for leaving.

I skated home that day, still breathless from my close encounter with Angie. All afternoon, her face had swum before my school books. It was a good job I knew about her private knockings with DJ Terry Tilson, or I might've really believed she found me interesting.

I needed a cold drink, and hoped there was some orange juice left. Dad normally used it as a vodka mixer. I went over to the fridge, but hardly dared put my hand on it. I didn't even recognize the thing. Was this a brand-new one? No, not unless all these types came with *The Razzler Rocks* etched across them. But the door had been scrubbed clean, and all the stripper girls were removed.

I yanked open the door, and fell back to the sink in shock. I must be in the wrong house! Our fridge was crammed full of the greenest, fruitiest, healthiest food that money could buy in Millom. It wasn't quite the weird stuff you got in Mum's shop (soba noodles, flaxseed meal, umeboshi vinegar) but it wasn't a bad effort.

Most of it was from the local Co-op or Somerfield. There was pure English apple juice; strawberry-banana smoothie; organic avocadoes, cabbages, carrots and bananas; blocks of tofu; weird mushrooms that looked poisonous; free-range eggs; big bunches of fresh basil and parsley.

The last time this fridge had seen fresh herbs was the day before Mum left.

I checked the kitchen cupboards, in case this miracle had spread further. Sure enough, they were filled with Fairtrade green tea; peppermint tea; jars of sugar-free peanut butter; organic brown rice; wheat-free pasta. *Wheat-free pasta?*

I gave in at that point and let my mind scramble wildly. And then . . . and then, of course! This could all mean only one thing. Mum had come back! At last she had forgiven Dad his many sins, decided we must be a family again, sold her house in Ulverston and come home. I raced upstairs, expecting to find her tidying the bedrooms, lighting incense in the bathroom and tutting at the mess on my floor.

'Mum!' I shouted, sprawling onto the landing. 'Mum! Where are you?'

I looked in my room. The set of bunk beds stood there, but nobody was about.

Finally I skipped towards Dad's room at the far end. I caught a whiff of lavender joss sticks. Mum was here somewhere, all right. But suppose she and Dad were having a . . . reunion? I tapped softly at the door. 'Mum?' I said. 'Are you there? Can I come in?'

There was no answer. Perhaps they were asleep in each other's arms. I needed to know for sure. I pushed the door gently.

The Razzler was lying alone on his bed. The carpet was clean, and all his music stuff was neatly stacked on the shelves. His tinted shades lay on a bedside table. I hardly knew my own father without them. Only his mad mohican haircut gave the game away. He stared unseeing at the ceiling, where a spider hung by a thread.

'Dad?' I said. 'What's going off? Where's Mum?'

There was no reply, not even a murmur. I was freaked out. I walked over to the bed and kicked its base. 'Dad? What gives? Huh?'

His lips parted, but the answer was a while in coming. 'Not now, Andy. I'm very tired. Leave me alone for a bit, please.'

I felt let down and empty. 'Well, has Mum been for a visit?' I asked. 'It's just that there's a load of nice stuff in the kitchen.'

Dad squeezed his face muscles tightly, like someone in agony. The whites of his eyes, normally hidden by those dark glasses, were ringed with red. He lay there lifeless, in T-shirt, jeans and black socks, like someone waiting to be measured for a coffin. I went downstairs and phoned Mum. I only got her answering machine. *'Hello, this is Jasmine. Please leave a message.'* Beeeep!

So I sat down at the spotless kitchen table and tried to do some school work. I kept listening for any sound from upstairs, a creak or a cry, but none came. An hour later, and Dad still hadn't come down. There was a knock on the door, more like a heavy thump, and I went to answer it. Seconds later I was outside Razzle's room.

'Dad,' I said. 'It's your Motor Heads group. They're waiting for you.'

No reply from within. 'Dad,' I said again, louder. 'The Motor Heads are waiting. Shall I tell them to go round the back? Is the garage locked?'

I pushed open the door. Dad still hadn't moved. He spoke very gently.

'Tell them I'm not free tonight,' he said. 'Just say I'm . . . indisposed.'

'Right. Um, they won't understand what that means.'

'In that case, just say I'm terribly sorry. So very sorry for everything.'

NINETEEN

Some of the Motor Heads got a bit narked at Dad's no-show that night. With nothing organized to do, they went off to Haverigg on their bikes, and rode across the bowling green there. Its green turf got all churned up, and cost the old folks who ran it a fortune to repair. That's how much that lot needed The Razzler. Without him around to give their bleak lives a bit of structure, they went right back off the rails.

Dad spent that evening alone in his room. I sat downstairs, listening to a silence that grew thunderous. There was none of his usual music to shake the floors and ceiling. No tuneless yowling in the shower as he got ready to go out. No late-night bashing of our stiff oven door as he reheated a takeaway. No early hours stumbling to the bathroom for a loud piddle.

I tried phoning Mum again, but she was still out. Thinking back to the weekend, I remembered how close she'd been to Abayakurti. He'd come back with us on Sunday afternoon, and was still there when I left for the bus home.

I even looked in the phone book, in case he'd got himself listed under 'Abayakurti'. In the end I gave up and went to bed quite early. A good job too, as Dad woke me up around seven o'clock with noise from the kitchen. I turned over to sleep again, but he called me ten minutes later.

'Andy? Breakfast!'

I groaned, and made a slow job of getting dressed and going down. At least he sounded back to normal. But my dad wasn't back to normal, he was far from it. Because laid out on the kitchen table was a spread like I'd never imagined here.

There was a dish of what looked like dodgy scrambled eggs, but was in fact scrambled tofu with turmeric spice. Brown bread in thick wedges, without butter. Slices of mango, drizzled with lime juice and fresh coriander. A steaming pot of ginger tea. Bowls of milky muesli. And a jug of what might well be liquidized seaweed.

'What's all this?' I said, mouth gaping.

'This?' said Dad, holding up the jug. 'It's cucumber avocado milkshake. With soya milk and brown-rice syrup.'

'I didn't mean that,' I said. 'I meant, what's all . . *this*? What the heck's going on?'

The Razzler stared at me as if I'd lost the plot. 'Nothing's going *on*,' he laughed. 'It's time to wise up and get a bit healthy. That's all. Sit. Eat. Let's go.'

I slowly pulled up a chair, as if being invited to dine with a maniac. None of the food tasted much different from a breakfast at Mum's place, but eating it here was like finding the Bronx Crew holding a seminar on Mozart.

'Is all this connected to your doctor's visit yesterday?' I asked.

Dad spooned up some muesli and paused to down his milkshake. 'Let's just say I got a slight warning,' he said, 'and leave it at that. I've neglected you for long enough, mate. Time I wised up, like I said.'

I poured out some of the herby tea. 'I'm sure Mum's gonna be pleased,' I said. 'Can't wait to tell her.'

'Ah,' said Dad. 'Actually, Andy, I'd rather you didn't tell her. She might sort of think it's all on account of her. You know how women are.'

'No,' I said. 'I don't.'

'You will. One day. And then you'll understand.'

As there'd been very few volunteers for Angie's poetry project, Mrs Longden had rounded up a number of school villains and forced them to take part. Maybe it was all part of Angie's punishment. They shuffled into the sports hall at break for the first rehearsal.

Angie looked so nervous. She even took off her glasses to avoid seeing some of the dregs that Mrs Longden had chosen. By the time she put them back on, people were slumped in the hall's four corners. I stood near the front, like a right little lapdog. I even handed out copies of Wordsworth's poem, as Angie's hands were shaking too much. She gave me a grateful smile, which made my stupid ears burn.

Angie tried to lift her voice over the bored chatter.

'Hi, everyone. Yeah, c-could you all . . . could you all come a bit closer? Hello? You at the back? Would you . . . would you mind just moving on down here? Thanks ever so. That's great. Fantastic.'

Some were lying down, some were half asleep, most looked fed up. But there was a brief silence when Angie began.

'OK, well, as you know, or maybe you don't but I'll tell you anyway, it's the two hundredth anniversary this year of when William Wordsworth wrote "Daffodils".'

'Who?' yelled some boy wearing a shoe on his head.

'William Wordsworth?' Angie said politely. 'A famous Cumbrian poet, yeah? Some of you might have been to Dove Cottage in Grasmere, where he lived.'

A girl with a black eye shouted, 'Is he the one who took loads of ecstasy and stuff?'

Angie's voice was already drying up. 'Umm, well he was known to have the odd pipe of something. I'm sure he was just trying to get inspired.'

'Smack head!' laughed the girl.

'Shut up,' I said, turning round. 'Just listen and learn.'

'Heck!' she screamed back. 'Hark at Mr Ear Ache. Just 'cos Diana Dowder's gone and dumped you.'

'OK, you guys!' Angie called out, almost drooping with desperation. '*Please* listen up. As you know, we're gonna be broadcast by the BBC for this reading. It's really important we all learn the poem off by heart, so we don't let the school down.'

A chorus of heavy sighs and groans broke out.

'Right,' said Angie. 'Now this poem was written by Wordsworth after he saw some flowers by Ullswater. It was on a stormy day and he was with his sister Dorothy.'

Someone farted so loudly that even I smiled. Angie fought on over the uproar.

'It was Dorothy's diary account of that day that inspired the poem. It was first published under the title, "I Wandered Lonely as a Cloud". William altered it later, and the second version is the one that's best known today. OK, so you all have a copy in front of you. Just listen first, while I read it through.'

She was brilliant and brave, I thought. Just amazing. Her face was scarlet with nerves and stress, but somehow she kept going. Then she began to read aloud, and it was like she was reciting one of her own poems to the world. Her voice was graceful and dreamlike, all ups and downs, all light and shade.

> 'I wandered lonely as a Cloud
> That floats on high . . . o'er Vales and Hills,
> When all at once . . . I saw a crowd . . .
> A host of golden daffodils;
> Beside the lake . . . beneath the trees,
> Fluttering . . . and dancing . . . in the breeze.'

By this point, some kids were giggling so much that I really feared one or two might wet themselves. Others lay flat, with the poem over their faces like a mask. Someone was even crunching a copy in his mouth. But I sat there enchanted, as if Angie's voice was a secret hypnotic signal. She reached the final verse, and its joyful closing couplet:

> *'And then my heart . . with pleasure fills,*
> *And dances . . . with the daffodils.'*

I gazed at her through brimming eyes. Someone else gave a snarling snore that sent the others off into dizzy fits. Angie floated back to reality after her poetic flight somewhere with Wordsworth. She saw the dull faces in front of her and got nervous again. I tried to catch her eye with a warm smile, but I sat there ignored.

'OK, guys,' she said. 'Um, let's all try reading it. From the top. Try and stay in time with me. Let's have a go together, after three. It starts, *I wandered lonely as a Cloud, That floats on high o'er Vales and Hills.* One . . . two . . . three . . .'

The grumpy chanting that followed was more like a foreign language.

> *'I wundud lurly . . . uza clow . . .*
> *Ut flerts on eye . . . or vells n illz . . .'*

Imagine listening to a load of murderers reading out their own death sentences. It was way more dismal than that. Finally, despite my brightest efforts, the group lumbered on to that closing couplet: *And then my heart with pleasure fills, And dances with the daffodils*. But this is how it grumbled across in the hall that day.

> *'Un themmy art . . . wiv . . . peshor fillz . . .*
> *And ances . . . wivver . . . dafferdillz.'*

Someone stood up. 'Can we go now? Break's nearly over.'

'Of course,' said Angie, all smiles. 'Thanks so much, everyone. Try and learn this off by heart, if you can. We don't want loads of rustling sheets during the BBC broadcast. We'll rehearse again on Friday break. If that's OK with you guys. Yes? No? Guys?'

Everyone piled out, totally ignoring Angie.

'And tell all your friends!' she shouted. 'We still need loads more readers.'

She paced around a bit, breathing deeply, her leggy limbs flashing. I followed the grumbling herd out, then paused at the main school door. I went back to the sports hall, trying to think of some excuse or something clever to say.

I didn't need to. Angie stood with her head against the white brick wall. Her hands were over her face, her shoulders shaking. I heard harsh sobbing, and went quietly over. I touched her shoulder.

'It'll be OK,' I said. 'You'll turn it around.'

She faced me with soggy cheeks. 'No, I won't!' she cried. 'Turn that lot around in time for the broadcast? Let alone find some vital insight into the world of daffodils. If only your granddad wasn't so ill . . .'

She left this hanging, like some hint of emotional blackmail.

'Yeah, he's fading fast,' I said. 'He told me at the week-end he's off to the sunless land. *From sunshine to the sunless land.* I think that's how he put it.'

Angie sniffed. 'That's by Wordsworth too,' she said. 'You funny boy. Full of little mysteries, aren't you?'

'Not really,' I said as the bell rang for end of break. 'No more than you.'

Angie wiped her eyes on a sleeve. 'Can't you ask your granddad if there's any way he can help?' she asked. 'I've got to find some stunning info on daffodils or else this whole project is a wreck. Maybe he knows someone else local who's an expert. Someone young, like you.'

I held my chin as if deep in thought. 'I can ask him,' I said. 'But don't bank on it.'

'I won't,' Angie sighed. 'But I'd love anyone for ever who could help me out of this mess. I'd love them with a passion!'

* * *

The Razzler did us proud at supper. We had grilled vegetables and wheat-free pasta with Thai peanut sauce. For pudding there was a peach sorbet with pineapple.

'You've been busy,' I said, my taste buds on fire.

'The work of the heart is a work of art,' Dad said.

I nearly choked on a roasted pepper. 'Blimey, Dad. What have you been reading?'

'The future,' he said. 'I've been reading the future. I now see how things must be.'

'Right,' I muttered. 'Not before time.'

Dad raised a glass of mango smoothie. 'Here's to Mother Nature,' he said.

TWENTY

I skated and loafed around Millom all night, just in the vain hope of seeing Angie somewhere. I wanted to be where she was, to breathe where she was breathing.

Having seen her acting strangely around the church-yard before, I rumbled on Orange Flyer down to the graves there. It was half past nine. I slipped between the tombs, reading the carved inscriptions on rows of headstones by moonlight. It was peaceful and tender among the dead. I sat quietly by the grave of some boy who'd gone to Granddad's 'sunless land' aged eleven. His date of death was fifteen years ago, around the time I was born.

Then someone came crunching quickly along the path. I hid behind a gravestone and watched Angie Hutchinson go down to where my daffodil heart lay blooming by Mr Tyson's grave. Angie knelt on the grass and closely inspected the flowers growing there. She looked right inside the trumpet parts and fondled the petals. Finally, with a quick pull, she yanked out one of those Mystics. Hiding it under her jacket, she stalked off the way she'd come.

I gave it five minutes, then followed, but she'd

vanished. Back off to the Cornflake estate, perhaps, and her big house lined with learning. I skated around some more, hoping for another glimpse of her, but I was thrilled enough just then. Angie Hutch had in her possession, clutched close to her breathing body, a daffodil that I had planted! It was almost like she was pressing *me* to her heart.

I'd love anyone for ever who could help me out of this mess . . . I'd love them with a passion.

That was what she'd said in the sports hall earlier. And it was me, Andrew Kindness, who held the key to Angie's happiness. All I had to do was come clean about my private passion for daffodils, help her make a triumph of this BBC thing, and be swept into sweet bliss for ever. Those were her own words. *For ever.* She'd promised it.

But reality soon clawed its way back in. Angie was getting sorted already, by a guy way older than me who had his own radio show. And what if I did come clean about my talent with daffodils, then got spat back by Angie when the BBC cleared off? I'd be left exposed as the supreme saddo who fiddled with flowers 'cos he couldn't make it with girls. Who liked sweet petals and posies, and planted Valentine shapes by dusty graves. I still maybe had two more years of schooling here. Maybe another year after that before I could escape the town, even if anywhere else would have me. Too thick for uni, too gloomy for a job. Too ugly for Angie . . .

By the time I reached home in our dusty street, I was

morbid. Dad was at the doorway looking out for me. He waved in relief.

'Getting late,' he said.

'Just out skating,' I said. 'Oh . . . Hey up, what's all this?'

Coming down the street towards us was Malky in his silver Porsche. He was driving very slowly, and the closer he got the louder we gasped. His precious Porsche had been brutalized. Nor did it look like a traffic accident. Someone – someone with nerves of rigid steel – had taken a crowbar to Malcolm Dowder's pride and joy. The headlights had been smashed in. The bonnet was bashed and scraped. The flanks were dented and scarred.

Malky pulled up outside our door. He got out with a grim smile, his cowboy boots clomping over concrete.

'Evening, Randolph,' he said. I was ignored, and shrank into the hallway.

'Er, evening, Malcolm. Had some trouble?'

Malky put on a breezy show, but you could sense the fury within.

'Aye, just a little. Some wide boys from up Whitehaven way who reckon I've been treading on their turf. But we know exactly what's what and who's who. We'll maybe pay them a visit for afternoon tea tomorrow.'

'I see,' Dad said. 'So, er, what can I do?'

'Fix this motor up, can you? Don't wanna take it down the garage in Barrow. They might check the licence plate and find it not quite . . . regular.'

'Ah, right,' said Dad, stroking his mohican. 'Not sure I've got all the right gear for this. You wanna park it round the back, and I'll see?'

'Will do,' said Malky. 'Oh, and there's one other thing, Randolph. You being such a handy man, and all.'

'Uh-huh?'

Malky came closer, his nose almost touching Dad's. 'Can you knock us up a few ingot moulds? You know the sort. Like those in the local museum.'

'Phew,' Dad said. 'Well, I possibly could. I might need an original to work from though.'

'Consider it done,' said Malky. 'Say about ... two dozen moulds? Soon as you can, my friend.'

Dad nodded glumly, aware he was getting dragged into something dodgy. Malky gave Dad's cheeks a firm friendly slap, then purred his Porsche into our back alley. Dad and me slunk inside to the kitchen, where he'd been busy squeezing oranges.

'What are ingot moulds?' I asked. 'Are they like those that Granddad used to talk about?'

'Aye,' said Dad. 'A relic from the iron-mining days. The hot metal got poured into ingot moulds and was left to set. They're like a fat square shape. Your granddad kept a few as souvenirs, but I wasn't gonna let Malky know that.'

'What's he want them for?'

'Heck knows,' Dad said. 'I can guess, but I'd rather stay ignorant. You want some fresh orange juice? It's organic, and fairly traded.'

* * *

I felt unclean after Malky's visit, and went round to my little garden. His battered Porsche blocked the alleyway and the garage entrance, so I had to squeeze by to get inside. The doorway in our garage had a big padlock. I slid the key in and went through, leaving the lock undone. Dad's own red sports car stood there, spotless. Then I slid the bolt aside from the back door and went through.

I had Granddad's scutcher with me. I dripped some water onto my patch of new cross-breed daffodils, the ones I had named Angie.

Thinking of her made me feel a little smoochy, and I held a Girl Friend daffodil to my face. It smelled so fresh and lusty. I had a little nibble of its yellow petals, like I was gently biting someone's lips. I got a sweet sting on my tongue, and went into a dreamy trance. I think I even spoke loving words to the Girl Friend, as if chatting it up.

I was so engrossed that I didn't hear the garage door creak behind me. With my back turned, I wasn't aware of someone creeping through. I never knew how long they stood there and stared. Only when I heard a loud cough did I snap out of this daze. And that's how Angie Hutchinson found me. Standing among flowers and bulbs, among soil and seeds, with a yellow-green flower to my lips.

TWENTY-ONE

'My, oh my,' said Angie, hands on her slender hips. 'So this is what you get up to in private. Can we all play?'

'Who let you in?' I demanded. 'How did you know I was here?'

Angie sat down on an upturned bucket. 'I've been spying on you all night,' she said. 'You seem to have a strange yen for churchyards. And daffodils.'

'What?' I said. 'So you knew I was watching when you stole that daffodil from Mr Tyson's grave?'

'Yep. I sure did. Thought it might draw you out of hiding, in righteous anger.'

I stared at her slim smug face. That reddish-blonde hair blew in strands over her cheeks. I knelt close by Angie and stared her out.

'Bit of a one for secrets yourself,' I said. 'What with DJ Terry Tilson, and all that.'

'That's nothing,' she said. 'I've met him socially a few times. That's all.'

'Is that so?' I said. 'Well, just for the record, it wasn't Martha Tinker and Stevo out on The Slaggy that night. Remember? The night you and Terry nearly turned his car over from the inside? It was just little me, collecting some daffodil bulbs for my granddad.'

Angie looked at me with a new regard. It was like she'd found out I wrote better poetry than her.

'Well, well,' she said. 'You're not quite as green as you look. Although you've clearly got green fingers. Were those your daffs up at the churchyard?'

'Yep. A bunch of Mystics. A cross-breed of my granddad's. I've just done a new species of my own. It's planted right there by the fence.'

'Right. And what's it called, this new one?'

I must've gone the colour of a plum tomato. 'Er, no name yet,' I lied. But there was a little white label tag over there, stuck in the soil where I'd sown the seeds. Before I could wrestle her to the ground, Angie had jumped over to it. She held up the plastic marker with *Angie* inked across. I closed my eyes and lay back on dewy grass in despair.

'I'm touched,' she said. 'Honest I am. That's so beautiful.'

I opened my eyes. She wasn't kidding. Angie looked close to tears.

'Why after me?' she asked.

'Why not?' I shrugged. 'We like the same music, I guess. And you must like daffodils to have read Wordsworth's poem out like that.'

Angie came and sat beside me. 'Yeah. I do like nice flowers. Daffs best of all. And what I need so bad right now is a total daffodil expert who goes to my school, who breeds these things in private, and who's ready to tell the whole world about it.'

And so Angie explained the full story behind Terry, Mrs Longden and the BBC broadcast, filling me in on the bits I didn't already know. By the end she was begging me to take part, and be interviewed live on air about my Girl Friends and King Alfreds.

'There's no way,' I said. 'I'll be a laughing stock around here. The boy with a pocketful of posies. No way!'

'But *listen*,' said Angie, clasping my arm tightly. 'Think of all the offers that might come your way. Just imagine.'

'Offers? What offers?'

'Oh, I dunno. Job offers, interview offers. Pretty girl offers, hmm?'

'More likely someone's gonna stick one on me for being a wimp. We ain't living in Keswick, y'know. It's not all teashops and tourists around here.'

Angie sighed and sat quietly. Finally she said, 'OK then, here's the ace up my sleeve. In a few days, me and Terry are driving down to Manchester for a rock gig. I'm telling Mum we're on a school trip to some Shakespeare play and I'm staying over at a friend's in Ulverston. How about coming along? You ever been to a real gig?'

Had I heck! The nearest I'd been to live music was Glastonbury highlights on BBC2.

The wind blew stronger, so we sat with our backs to the garage.

'I'd love to,' I said. 'So who are we gonna see?'

'Ah. That's a surprise. But it'll be good and loud, I promise. Terry gets free tickets for north-west events. I told him there might be a third person for this one.'

'Wow. So, what you're saying is, you get me into a top rock gig and in return I make the BBC thing happen?'

'That's the size of it,' said Angie. 'But what about your dad? Won't he worry if you're out all night?'

'He'll not notice,' I said. 'Though he has been acting strangely of late.'

Angie stood up, brushing earth off her bum. 'Hmm. Well, it's worth taking a risk. I'll let you know the wheres and whens. Do we have a deal?'

A night on the town with Angie. An evening in the company of my favourite DJ. Shame they both came together, but there was time yet. Maybe on the night I could let slip Angie's true age and identity. Watch DJ Terry storm away, and be there to pick up the pieces.

'Deal,' I said. Angie held out her hand, which I shook. Her fingers were warm and soft. I imagined what else they might touch. My brain went into meltdown.

She opened the garage's back door and she was gone, leaving me hurt and happy, and shamed and crushed, and wildly alive. How could one girl create such a crisis inside you? I felt like skating away for miles, to burn off the fever that grew with each second.

Just imagine where all this could lead! I pictured me and Angie, the toast of Millom and the BBC, after an amazing Wordsworth poetry event. She'd be in love with my sweetly tragic life. She'd ache for a boy a year younger than herself. No more would she need an older guy, with his fast car and free gig tickets. She would desire a return to innocence. We would be everything to each other. And my Angie cross-breed daffodils would become an icon of purest love.

'You OK, Andy?' asked Dad later.

I sat with head in hands at the kitchen table. Now I felt all moody and grouchy again. I was high, then low, like a boy on a trampoline.

'Just peachy,' I muttered. 'What's that you're making?'

'Chestnut pilaf with black rice,' Dad said. 'For my lunch tomorrow.'

'You're really going for this healthy thing, aren't you?'

'To fully transform is a slow process,' he said. 'Better late than never.'

TWENTY-TWO

I awoke in the early hours of Wednesday morning. A wave of sweet sorrow stabbed my heart. It settled into a dull and drowsy ache. Somewhere behind my eyes, a swell of tears was trying to crash through. I imagined The Blocks by the beach at Millom, letting the tide break among their great concrete cubes. I dreamed up scenes of great joy, always with me and Angie at the centre. Then came the more likely visions, the ones with a tragic end. I couldn't get back to sleep, and flopped about under the duvet for ages.

I knew what great drama lay behind all this pain. I was in love.

Dad came in to shake me awake about eight o'clock. I felt all sweaty and glum. But seconds later, with my radio blasting something rowdy, I was dying to get out and share my new passion with the world.

I raced through Dad's lovingly made breakfast of sugar-free blueberry muffins, vegan pancakes and tropical fruit smoothie.

'Terrific,' I mumbled, mouth crammed.

'What's got into you?' he asked. 'You look on fire.'

'Nuffink,' I said, swallowing hard. 'Got a full day, that's all.'

'Aha,' Dad said. 'Me too. So let us end this meal with a prayer of thanks.'

My head thrust out. '*What?*' I said.

Dad's eyes were already closed, his mouth muttering, his hands clasped. I watched him, still believing he'd crack up laughing any second. But he didn't. He just went upstairs and shut himself in the bathroom. I heard a CD playing some soft classical music. I was worried enough right then to phone Mum again. A man answered.

'Hello?'

'Oh. Hi. Who's that?'

'It's Abayakurti. Is that Andrew?'

'Yeah. Is my mum there?'

'She's in meditation right now. Can I help?'

'Er, no. Just say I need to talk to her. Thanks. Bye.'

'Oh, Andrew?' said Abayakurti.

'Yeah?'

'Have you given any more thought to our little chat last Sunday?'

My body shrank into itself. 'Um, no, not really. Gotta go, Abayakurti.'

'Because that Horny Goat Weed you were looking at contains quite a powerful dose. You'd be far better off taking a mild blend of Korean Ginseng and Dong Quai.'

My face had gone limp. 'I would?'

'Yes, Andrew. Or even Ashwagandha. It's been used

as a stimulus for sexual desire since one thousand BC. Just so you know.'

'OK, fab. There goes the front door. Cheers.'

'A blessing be—'

I whammed the phone down, breathing out heavily and shaking my head.

That afternoon we went on an English trip to the Forum 28 arts centre in Barrow. Some local children's writer had a new book out, and we zoomed off in a coach to hear him yakking. He'd even gone to the trouble of setting up a slide show to go with his reading. But the balding hulk who did IT at the Forum was clueless. He messed about with a projector while we shouted with kids from other schools in the little lecture theatre.

In the end the author gave up, called for order and just read. It wasn't bad, actually, and we lined up after to get our homework diaries autographed. One girl wanted her detention note signing, and someone gave him a fag packet to scrawl on.

But it was on the way home that a real moment of madness came. At least for me. Miss Williams, our young and long-haired English teacher, took the scenic route back. We went along the coast road towards Ulverston, passing the beach where I'd failed to remain very long on the sands last Sunday. I even saw that same aimless gang as before, swinging a baseball bat at any stray sea creature.

The coach braked suddenly, throwing everyone aside. A car had turned left in front of us without warning. It sped down the quiet lane leading towards the Buddhist temple at Conishead Priory.

'Idiot!' shouted Miss Williams, her mane of hair flapping.

The other kids were making a big show of picking themselves off the floor. So it was only me who got a good look at the fast vehicle and its driver. My face went hard against the window in shock.

I suppose I could have been mistaken. Only you don't mistake your dad for anyone else, do you? Especially when he's got a fiery mohican, tinted shades, and drives a red open-top sports car. Not much room for error there.

What the heck was he doing down at the priory? I imagined some sort of bizarre triangle between Dad, Mum and Abayakurti. Maybe the priory rented out rooms for such karmic love matches. This was all getting way beyond me.

Before we got off the bus, Miss Williams reminded us about the Wordsworth anniversary poem project.

'And we still need loads more readers,' she called out. 'The BBC are expecting a proper massed reading of "Daffodils", not a few dozen snorts and grunts. Please see Angela Hutchinson, lower sixth, if you'd like to take part. Mrs Longden might yet swoop down and grab a few more of you lot. Why not save her the trouble?'

I hadn't seen Angie all that day, though my poor soul cried out for any glimpse. I hung about on Orange Flyer after school as the crowds parted around me. At about half past four I'd almost given up when she came out of the main entrance.

She gave me a smile that stirred up last night's emotional torments. 'Hi there,' she said. She came closer and whispered, 'You OK for Friday night?'

A shiver of thrills kicked in. 'Friday?' I said. 'Is that for definite?'

'Sure is,' said Angie. 'Terry's Friday show is pre-recorded some weeks. No need to tell you it's total hush-hush. One word in the wrong ear and we're all sunk.'

'I won't tell,' I said. 'So, who are we gonna see? Someone mega? Is it at the Manchester Evening News Arena? Is it a sell-out?'

Angie smiled. 'I won't spoil the surprise,' she said. 'Just remember your part of the deal. I get you into a proper gig, and you come clean to the world on BBC day.'

I didn't like being reminded this was all just a bargain. It didn't fit with my passionate desire for Angie. But this was the first step. I'd be there for the long haul.

'I like your woolly hat thing,' she said. 'Dead cute. I like the long flaps.'

'Oh, thanks,' I said, staring down at my worn skate-board. 'My mum made it.'

'Yeah? Wish *my* mum had cool taste in fashion. I mean, look at this blazer.'

'Mmm,' I said. 'So is that why you steal clothes from the church's jumble sale donations?'

She leaned forward, rosy mouth gaping. 'Whaaat?' she said. 'You . . . little flaming spy! When did . . .? I mean . . . where . . .?'

'I just worked it out,' I said. 'I saw you grabbing a nice leather jacket out of a bin liner one time. There were loads of sacks by the church door. All for the spring jumble sale. Guess a girl's gotta get her gear where she can.'

Angie stepped back, arms folded, and tossed her hair.

'I can see you're not one to fool with,' she said. 'Any more surprises?'

I wobbled on Orange Flyer. 'I'm sorry,' I said. 'I just think you and me are alike, what with our private lives that people don't know about.'

Angie began walking down the hill away from school. I picked up my board and followed. She spoke to me quietly, in confidence.

'This whole poetry thing I do was my mum's plan,' she said. 'I'd no idea I could be any good at it. Or maybe everyone else is just rubbish. I'd much rather write rock lyrics and front a band. But I can't see my mum, the High Sheriff of Cumbria, forking out for guitar lessons. And my dad's just a boring man who hides in the corner.'

I smiled, and allowed myself to touch her hair. I said, 'I only took up with daffodils after what happened to me six years ago. I just wanted to stay clear of the bay.'

Angie nodded as we reached the turning for her house on the Cornflake estate. 'Did you ever talk about it with anyone?' she asked.

'Just my parents, mostly,' I said. 'But what could anyone say? It wasn't my fault and I tried to fetch help. I've never felt safe, even on solid ground, ever since. It's like the whole earth is just waiting to pay me back somehow. Just waiting for one chance to pull me under.'

Angie played with my woolly hat flaps. 'It'll pass one day,' she said. She kissed her fingers and pressed them to my forehead. 'Until Friday,' she said.

'Yeah,' I breathed, watching her walk away. My legs collapsed so quickly with longing for Angie that I feared those quicksand nightmares were upon me again.

TWENTY-THREE

Malky's battered Porsche was still blocking our alley and garage. There was no sign that Razzle had started working on it yet.

I made a cup of tea, and heard Dad moving about on the upstairs landing.

'Cup of tea, Dad?' I shouted up

'Aye, cheers,' he called back. 'Cup of detox.'

'Cuppa what?'

'A cup of detox.'

A cup of *what*? Detox? *Deeee*tox? I still couldn't get over all this. It was like hearing Dracula ask for organic milk. I rooted in the cupboard for a box labelled DETOX TEA. It sounded like that Detto stuff we cleaned the toilet with. Smelled a bit like it too. I took Dad's mug upstairs.

'OK, Razzle,' I said. 'Here's your cup of botox.'

'*De*tox, you prat.' He sipped and scowled. 'And you don't put rotten sugar in good stuff like this.'

'But you always have four sugars. And proper tea with fatty milk.'

'Not any more. I can't drink this with sugar in. A drop of organic honey, maybe.'

'We haven't got any. Have we?'

'There's three jars by the sink. I'll sort it.' And he was away downstairs, leaving me to scratch my head and wonder.

By Thursday afternoon a brand-new juicer had appeared at home. A few weeks back, this would've been like spotting blue whales in the Duddon estuary. But in our squeaky-clean kitchen these days, it was hardly noticed. And still Malky's Porsche stood out the back in tatters.

I unlocked the garage and went in for a look around. Was Dad doing any work at all right now? I found his window-cleaning cloths in a dry bucket, all stiff and stale. There'd not been a drop of wet froth on them in days. Nor had the Motor Heads called round for their weekly workshop session.

I went back inside and found Dad sitting cross-legged on the living-room floor. His eyes were closed. There was a slim book beside him. He was listening to something really chilled. As I barged in, he gazed up and whisked the book under the couch.

'Gave me a shock,' he said. 'Never heard you come back.'

'What you hiding under there?' I asked. 'Is that a naughty novel?'

'No, you daft prune. Slob off.'

'Ah, go on. Let me look.' I tried to kick the thing out from beneath the sofa.

'I said, *leave* it,' Dad snapped. 'It's nothing for you.'

'OK, OK,' I said, my hands held up. 'Just wanted to ask when Malky's car might be fixed. It's kind of blocking the path.'

Dad sat still, his face clenching. 'There's too many bad vibes around that car,' he said. 'It's not healthy for me to touch criminal property.'

'I see,' I said. 'And what about those ingot moulds he was asking for? Are you gonna knock those up?'

'Same again,' Dad said. 'It's not positive work, helping that maniac. Let him whistle for them.'

There was a bang at the door. I went to answer. And there stood Malky the maniac, come to whistle for his mended car and ingot moulds. His tight white trousers, lined with sequins, were tucked into cowboy boots. He didn't look in a whistling mood.

'Your old man about?'

'Er, n-no, Mr Dowder. He's in . . . in town.'

'Town? Which town?'

'Um, in Barrow, I think. Is there a message?'

'Yeah. Tell him I want the car done by tomorrow. And no need for the ingot moulds now. I've got a stash from somewhere else. That all clear?'

'Y-yes, Mr Dowder. Thank you very much.'

I relayed the message back to Dad. 'Nice one, kidder,' he said. 'Ain't no chance of the car being repaired, though. I'll spin him some line about spare parts out of stock.'

'Wonder where he got those ingot moulds,' I said.

Dad laughed, and stood up with a painful wince. 'The likes of Malky can get what they want *when* they want,' he said. 'Probably stole the lot from a local museum.'

Dad went out very early on Friday. And just before leaving for school, I heard the postman call by. A brown doley type of envelope came through with Dad's name on. I stared at it, and slowly realized what might be going on with him. He'd never had anything sent from the social security before. He'd always made his own way in life, keeping clear of the benefit system and government handouts.

So *that* was it, I thought. He'd had to declare himself bankrupt, after years of overspending on junk food, booze and fags. That might explain the yoga – an attempt at finding peace in the midst of chaos. But it didn't account for his new diet. Surely no one who was bankrupt could afford to spend a pile on organic food.

I thought of that book I'd seen Dad hiding in the living room yesterday. Was it still there? I walked through, knelt down and felt below the settee. There it was, hiding among dust and crumbs. I pulled it out, sat back against the sofa and looked at the cover. Its front had one large letter C in the centre, so it took me a minute to work out the full title. Even then, my brain tried to reject the info it received.

This was the book I'd found under there:

C: Because Cowards Get Cancer Too by John Diamond.

There was a press quote below, describing it as 'urgent and funny'. *Phew*, that was OK then! Just a bad-taste comedy novel. So why had my dad hidden it? I read the back cover's blurb.

Part journal, part medical enquiry, this bestselling book is the everyday story of cancer. Of what cancer is, what it does, how it kills, how it can be cured.

I flicked wildly through the pages. I kept seeing words like 'hospital', 'diagnosis', 'X-ray', 'radiation', 'patient' and 'lump' come leaping out.

My fingers were shaking as I tugged at a leaflet stuffed between the pages. It looked like the sort you found in Mum's wholefood shop. Its headline was GERSON THERAPY. The printed words were a blur, but I worked out it had some link to curing cancer with a vegan diet. About soaking the human cells in natural goodness. A whole healing process, based on the mind and body working together.

I flung the book across the room and sat back in terror. I didn't care if cowards got cancer. Other people's dads got cancer, not mine. Not my crazy Razzler, with all his life and soul. Cancer took old and crabby people who had no hope left.

I sat there, hunched on the floor, for a long time. School had started, the working day had begun, but Andrew Kindness was unable to join in. I didn't move a muscle for ages, my head spinning with stormy thoughts.

Finally I looked up and saw spring sunshine flooding

the room. I realized it was Friday, and the day of my date with Angie, DJ Terry and a mega gig in Manchester.

It was also the morning of Angie's second rehearsal of Wordsworth's 'Daffodils'. I arrived at school just in time for break, so dazed that I'd walked all the way and left Orange Flyer at home.

I stood numbly in the sports hall, as even fewer of the school's debris than last time dragged themselves in. At least some of Angie's classmates had come along this time, in sympathy. She didn't seem to have many close friends. But even when Angie urged us to 'feel the words and their true meaning', I couldn't rise to it.

I heard the mumbling and chanting of poetry around me. It was better than last time, but still a long way from performance standard. And the whole thing needed a lot more voices involved.

After the rehearsal I went walking out with my head low. Angie called me over.

'Hi,' she said softly. 'You OK?'

I nodded, staring at her dull black shoes.

'Hmm. Well, tonight we can pick you up around six. On the beach road by The Blocks. That good with you?'

I whispered, 'Yeah. Whatever.'

Angie tugged my chin so our eyes met. 'Strange boy,' she said. 'You'll come alive tonight. I'm sure.'

My eyes filled up and I had to leave. I was madly in

love, and also in great fear for my dad. Try handling those two emotions together on a sunny spring Friday.

I went to the library at lunch time just to be near Angie and feel her comforting presence. I browsed my copy of *Kerrang!*, looking through the tour date adverts near the back. None of the major acts listed was on at the Manchester Evening News Arena that night. Nor at the Apollo either. It must be some top act whose tour was sold out, so there was no point placing ads for it now.

After school I finally spoke to Mum. I just needed to hear that loving voice. I didn't mention what I'd learned about Dad. It didn't seem fair until I knew a bit more.

'How's Granddad?' I asked. 'Is he picking up yet?'

There was a long silence. 'Andy, he's not good. He's been taken into hospital with breathing problems. I think he might be close to the end now, and he wants to see you – he keeps asking for you. Can you get over here tonight, love?'

TWENTY-FOUR

I'd never been so torn up over anything. If my granddad was dying then I had to be there. If my dad was very ill, then I should stay at home. If I couldn't think of anything but Angie Hutchinson, I must be somewhere close to her. In the end, I caved in to love and lust, foolish though I knew my dream probably was. I told Mum I'd be over first thing tomorrow, then went to find Dad in his room. He was lying down and resting, as he seemed to be all the time now.

'Dad,' I said, 'I'm going round to see some mates tonight. Might be back late. Don't wait up for me.'

'I won't,' he said. 'I'll be turning in early. I've made some eggless frittata and pineapple salad. It's in the fridge.'

'So I saw,' I said. 'Looks great.'

'Cheers.' He closed his eyes, the tinted shades folded beside him.

I lingered by the door. 'Dad?' I said quietly.

'Hmm?'

'You're the best,' I said. 'The best ever.'

He smiled, eyes still shut, and waved gracefully. 'You too, son,' he said. 'Have a wild evening.'

'I can stay here . . . if you like. Keep you company?'

'Nah. Glad you're making some friends. You go for it.'

I spent longer getting changed that evening than ever before. I washed my hair with Dad's new hemp and meadowsweet shampoo. I even ironed my black T-shirt and blue jeans, then cleaned my trainers. Nothing I could do about my ears, but taking the woolly hat was just drawing attention to them. And having walked to school that day without Orange Flyer, I felt safe leaving my faithful skateboard behind.

I walked through the quiet little town towards the beach. On stony ground, not far from a line of old railway sheds, stood a grubby caravan. It must be one of Malky's dealing dens. As I got nearer, some wasted-looking lad overtook me. He was dressed in black, with punky chains and a haircut like an exotic bird. His face was white and bony. He looked spaced out, and tripped over a few rocks. As he did so, some jewellery spilled from his pocket. A gold watch on a chain, several rings, a necklace and a large bracelet. He gathered up the bits and stuffed them back in, never once looking over at me. After stumbling to the caravan, with its drawn curtains and yellow light, he knocked six times. The door creaked open and the druggy punk went inside.

I crept as close as I dared, and listened. Not a sound from within. After several minutes, that darkly dressed punk emerged from the caravan clutching a plastic packet. He groped his way through a fresh breeze in the direction of town, and the railway station.

Then somebody twitched a caravan curtain and saw me there spying. I legged it away, splashing through puddles of red dirt water.

I stopped by The Blocks, heart thumping, and sat on the sea wall's gigantic dice. I looked across the deathly estuary. The mountains beyond it stared back, their wrinkled faces frowning. And then a car pulled up, which I recognized as Terry's from that night he was here with Angie. The leggy love of my life jumped out and ran across to me. She was dressed in a leather mini skirt, white trainers and red jacket. Her hair had some blue dye massaged into it. No sign of her glasses either.

'Hiya,' I said, looking her over. 'Good pickings in the jumble donations?'

'Uh-huh,' she said. 'Some of it almost brand new. Now listen up. You're actually my little brother and you've just got back from a school trip. I'm studying web design and graphic arts at Lancaster Uni. Our parents got divorced last year, so we live with our dad who's in finance. Oh, and I'm also twenty years old. Got all that?'

'Right,' I said. 'Got it. Erm, do I keep my real name?'

'Of course. So do I. Now come and meet Terry.'

DJ Terry Tilson raised his knuckles to mine. 'Hi, bro,' he said. 'Ready to rock?'

'Sure thing,' I said, feeling brighter than I had all day. 'I love your show. Listen to it both nights every week.'

'Cool, cool,' said Terry, starting up the engine. 'Right, we've just got one more person to pick up, then we hit the road.'

I felt a bit sad that someone else was coming. I hoped wildly it was Terry's real girlfriend or something, and that Angie was just tagging along. To my absolute misery, Terry turned down the rough track leading to Malky's gloomy gothic mansion. It stood almost atop the bay. No lights were on behind the dark windows. A bald bulky guy like a Buddhist bouncer was pacing around speaking into a mobile. And then the boss-eyed bruiser himself appeared from the front door. He was carrying a large rucksack which looked heavy. I didn't dare ask what was going on, or how Terry knew Malky. Angie didn't look surprised, but sat there sifting CDs.

Malky nodded at Terry, who handed him a key through the window. Malky went round the back, opened the boot and threw his rucksack in. It made such a heavy clunk that the whole car sagged for a second. We all looked up in surprise. Malky shifted the rucksack about a bit, slithering the heavy load here and there. It sounded like he'd got a few building bricks to use on someone or something later. Finally he was satisfied, closed the boot and got in beside me.

It's like I wasn't even there. He chucked a few of Terry's maps off the seat, most of them landing on me. I clearly wasn't forgiven for The Razzler's failure to mend his car on time. Perhaps he also knew that Diana had traded me in for Jason Brindley, so I was of no use or interest any more. He sat back, not using his seatbelt, and lit a cigar.

'Manchester, then,' said Malky. 'You can drop me off in the northern quarter. Pick me up later, when you've all had your little fun.'

At least he wasn't coming to the gig with us. But my dreams of a road journey with just Angie and Terry (despite my jealousy of him) had taken a dent. Having Malky there was like holding a house party for your mates, with your parents watching *Newsnight* in the living room.

Terry stuck on some Chili Peppers, mixed in with a bit of REM. I began to cheer up, and we wound down the windows in the warm evening. Gusty breezes blew in and ruffled our hair. Malky sat back and nodded off, despite the racket coming from four speakers. Angie looked round at me and smiled. Terry passed me a warmish bottle of Budweiser. I sipped it very slowly, having never forgotten the disaster that Mrs Tyson saved me from on that school trip to Grasmere. It was beyond all question that such a thing could happen with Angie around.

Terry drove at some speed from the Duddon estuary, and headed for the wild acres towards Ulverston. Soon we were beyond the boundary of the Lake District National Park. The sun was setting over the hills. Mountains faded away – range by rosy-red range. I felt a pang of sorrow to watch them go, like I was leaving for ever. I sat up straight, craning my neck for each last glimpse of spiked ridges.

We left Cumbria behind and the motorway opened out. I loosened up a bit and took a small sip of warm beer. I watched Angie singing and smoking. I was living at last!

TWENTY-FIVE

I tried to get a hint about who we were going to see that night from the CDs that Terry was playing. But they were mostly compilations, and snatches of his own radio shows.

'How's that beer doing?' he shouted, over the roar of music and open windows.

I raised the nearly full bottle with a grin. 'Just great, Terry!' I yelled back.

'Good, good!' he bawled back. 'Now you're seventeen, it's nearly all legal!'

I choked on the quick swig I'd taken. Seventeen? Angie had told him I was *seventeen*? I hardly looked the fifteen I actually was.

Malky awoke and tapped Terry's shoulder. We were approaching a motorway service station south of Bolton in Lancashire.

'Pull over here,' Malky ordered.

Without a word, Terry got into the slow lane and veered into the services. Maybe he was a bit nervous, as he missed the lane leading to the car park and drove into the area where those enormous trucks go. He also went in the wrong way. One of the great juggernauts came head-on towards us. Its headlights flashed like dragon's eyes. It seemed ready to swallow our tiny car. The driver hooted a deafening blast of horn. The left side of Terry's vehicle got scraped by the truck. Malky cursed quietly until Terry managed to park safely in the right place.

'You lot stay here and keep guard,' Malky said. He let himself out, taking his flashy mobile. We watched him wander off, barking orders into the phone.

'Wonder what's in that rucksack,' Angie said, looking past me over her shoulder.

Terry smiled. 'Couple of dead bodies?' He grinned. 'The head of some copper who got too close to Malky's dealings?'

I worked up the courage to join in. 'I saw some druggy type earlier,' I said. 'He had a load of jewellery, heading for a dodgy caravan near the old railway sheds.'

Terry shook his head. 'Bad business,' he said. 'Poor sod. Probably got so desperate for a hit that he nicked all his mum's precious things. If you ain't got the money to score, they'll take anything else you've got.'

'How do you know Malky?' I asked quietly, the music now turned low.

Terry shrugged. 'Who *doesn't* know Malky?' he said. 'He rang me up earlier demanding I take him to Manchester. I said I was going down there anyway. He said he *knew* that, which is why he was asking. It's like he knows your own private life before it's even been planned.'

Malky returned with coffee and fresh fags for himself, but nothing for us. We drove off again, heading south towards Greater Manchester. Terry turned the music back up. Angie was sitting right in front of me, her blue-blonde hair spilling over the back of the seat. I wondered where she'd managed to dye it, away from her mother's prying eyes. What a game of risk she was forever playing!

I saw Malky watching her with a sly grin. I guess he knew what was going on between Angie and Terry, but couldn't care less. Maybe he was keeping quiet until he could use it against one of them in some way.

Malky's presence was like a bad odour that nobody likes to mention. His wonky eye looked darkly at me, like it was my fault that Dad couldn't be bothered to repair that stupid Porsche.

I thought about my dad, lying alone at home with his illness that I really knew nothing about. He hadn't seemed too down these past few days, apart from that first night when I came home to find the house and fridge all spruced up. Maybe it was just a health scare and he was reading a book about cancer as a warning. I sent him a nice text:

HEY RAZZLE, ISN'T LIFE JUST GREAT SOMETIMES!?

He sent one back straight after:

SURE IS. I INTEND TO LIVE A LONG AND HAPPY ONE! OFF TO

BED NOW. DON'T MAKE A NOISE LATER AND WAKE ME!! HAVE
FUN WITH YOUR PALS! RAZZ.

That sounded good. I sat back happily, and tried not
to breathe Malky's putrid cigar smoke. But even his
presence couldn't take the shine off my growing excite-
ment. As we saw Manchester's crowded skyline creeping
up, I got all jittery. Then we saw the first road sign pointing towards the Manchester Evening News Arena. That
must be where we were headed. One of the north's
biggest venues, holding thousands of seats, offering a
massive stage for the world's top names to perform on.
Again, I tried to remember who was touring right now,
and who'd released a new album in the past few months
that they'd be out on the road promoting.

Terry ignored the signs for the MEN Arena and took
the route for Victoria Station instead. I spoke up in case
he'd missed it by accident.

'This isn't the way to the Evening News Arena,' I
protested.

Nobody said anything. Angie's face was turned
towards the window and she'd gone a bit red. Terry gave
her a quick glance and frowned. Malky chuckled, like I'd
cracked some joke that he approved of. All the road signs
became a blur from this point. I saw big notices for the football grounds at Old Trafford or the City of Manchester
Stadium. It was too early in the year for those giant outdoor
gigs that were sometimes held in such places.

'Hang a right here,' said Malky. Terry turned down the music as if awaiting further instructions. His little square of fuzzy beard was wobbling.

'Left at the top of Deansgate,' said Malky. 'Keep going . . . keep going . . .'

We passed the coach station on somewhere called Shudehill, and went slowly through darkened streets. I felt scared for the first time that journey, and wanted Orange Flyer there to cuddle.

'Take the first right,' said Malky. Terry followed these directions like he was a taxi driver.

'OK, just here,' said Malky as we slowed to a halt by the pavement. We were in a dimly lit back street, with a few sleazy shops all shuttered up. Malky got out, went round the back with Terry's keys and took out his rucksack. The car seemed to lift a little without its heavy load. Malky hitched the backpack onto his shoulders, which looked strange against his expensive suede overcoat.

He poked his head in at the window. 'Meet me here no later than two,' he said. Terry nodded and wound up the window. I felt a bit shocked. Two in the morning? We wouldn't be home until nearly daybreak. But at least Malky was finally out of the car, and we three could speed happily along to the gig.

Terry seemed to know the roads through Manchester pretty well. My face was pressed against the window as I watched this unreal world go by. Crowds of students, crowds of gorgeous girls, crowds everywhere. Bright lights in restaurants, flashy bars, big buildings, clothes shops, coffee shops, giant concrete car parks. And more people than I thought could ever live together in one place without them all going mad.

Terry turned towards Piccadilly Station, with its great glass roof and long slope leading up to the entrance. We went round the back, into what looked like a dead zone of the city. Gloomy brick buildings, shadowy streets, a few rundown pubs, and women dressed in skimpy clothes on the street corners. One of them caught my gaze through the window and gave me a shocking smile of thick lipstick. She wore a leopardskin coat. I stared through the back window after her. She leaned towards me, lips pursed up, and stroked her black-stockinged thighs.

Terry stopped the car by a big ugly pub on a corner. I could hear music blasting out from an upstairs room. The pavement was full of teenage guys in denim jackets, bikers wearing leathers, girls in tight trousers.

Terry parked behind a row of motorbikes and sat quietly for a moment. Angie chewed her nails and stared at the people outside. I wanted to know why we'd stopped here. There wasn't time to go for a drink if we wanted to reach the MEN Arena. It was already after eight o'clock. The support band would be on soon.

I tried reading the name on the pub sign hanging outside, but it was too old and filthy. All I could make out was the faded remains of a painted crown. Terry looked at me and Angie in turn. He touched Angie's blushing face with a hairy finger. She forced a quick smile.

It started to rain suddenly, and people hurried back into the dirty noisy pub.

'OK, guys,' Terry said. He sounded tired. 'Here we finally are. You ready to rock? Let's roll.'

TWENTY-SIX

I got out in a daze of disappointment. It turned swiftly into outrage. As Terry was locking the car, I ran up to Angie, who had already wandered off. I grabbed her elbow.

'What's going on?' I hissed angrily. 'You promised me a *real* gig.'

Angie folded her arms, her mouth twisting. 'This is a proper gig,' she said.

'What?' I cried. 'In this dodgy little place? I thought we were going to the MEN Arena.'

Angie tutted as if I was a silly child. 'Ah, heck,' she said. 'Who wants to see some tired old lags strutting their stuff on the stadium circuit? This is cutting-edge music here. It's about new bands on the way up. You can say you saw them first when they strike it big.'

She had the grace to blush as I stared her out. 'Right,' I said as Terry strolled towards us, his black bomber jacket sparkling. 'So, what great new stars are we here to see?'

'There's three bands on,' Angie said. As Terry caught up with us, she smiled and her voice turned excited. It was clear she'd been fooling him about what 'little brother' was expecting of this gig. 'Sounds like the first support act are on now. They're kinda emo-ish, from Wigan. Then there's a melodic hardcore band, down from Lancaster. And headlining are this Kendal group who Terry's featuring on the radio next week. They're called Seven Seals. A bit trippy, a bit punky, big melodies. That right, Terry?'

'That's about it,' he said. 'And we're all on the guest list. Let's get in.'

I nudged Angie's ribs. 'You mean we've come all this way to see a band from Cumbria?' I said. 'No chance!'

She pulled me along. 'Just shut up and enjoy it. You'll thank me later.'

There was a crowded bar downstairs, where they served pints in plastic glasses. Despite my huge feelings of anticlimax, I got a buzz from the pounding sounds above and the beery noise everywhere. Terry and Angie went to the bar and came back with a pint each and a Coke for me.

'Sorry, kidder,' said Terry. 'There's a bouncer on the door upstairs. Might want ID as you're only seventeen.'

'That's OK,' I said. 'I don't drink much. The odd bottled beer maybe.'

'Uh-huh. Maybe we can sort one for you later.'

We went up some dusty wooden stairs. Slops of spilled beer made my shoe soles all sticky. A thuggish hulk was guarding the way in at the top. The music was deafening from here. This bloke with a crooked nose nodded at Terry, who held up three fingers. Our hands got stamped on the back and we were in.

As you went into the spacious upstairs room, the stage was down the far end on the left. Each side of it was filled with a trembling stack of amps. I almost covered my large ears. The place was a storm of guitars, drums, bass, singing and shouted chatter all around.

I began to smile. Just being among so much noise and so many loved-up strangers felt pretty good. Even though it was a strange environment, not once did I get waves of nerves about the floor dissolving into quicksand. That cheered me too. Life was picking up for Andrew Kindness, I thought. Maybe I'd even tell Dad about tonight. He wouldn't be angry. It might help to make him feel better.

When I looked into the dark sea of bodies behind me, Terry and Angie had vanished. But I didn't care just then. That emo lot from Wigan were good. I began to bounce around a bit, and went closer to the front. The floppy-haired vocalist shook sweat from his fringe, his face a mask of pain as he sang. They got an encore, a slow ballad on acoustic guitars that made me long to have Angie close by.

I didn't go looking for her, in case she and Terry were throbbing together by the back wall. So I sipped my Coke and watched the roadies get things ready for the next lot. I was the smallest and youngest person there, but nobody hassled me. There was a big sign up, saying, ANYONE

CAUGHT USING OR DEALING DRUGS WILL BE HANDED OVER TO THE POLICE.

That made me feel safer too. And I was getting pretty high on life until the Lancaster hardcore lot came on. It was a barrage of noise, an attack on all your senses. Not a single note of melody anywhere, and the kind of naff guitar riffs even I could've played.

I slipped away from the front and mingled at the back, where I saw Angie and Terry. They seemed to be having a row, which left me quite happy. They stood apart, taking it in turns to yell in each other's ears. Terry was shaking his head and Angie was looking at the dark ceiling. I hugged myself with joy. Angie walked away in the end, taking a big swig of her pint.

Terry saw me and came over. He shook his head sadly. He shouted, 'Your sister can be pretty stubborn!'

I nodded, and blushed into my Coke.

Terry went on, 'I was just saying, she should come to the Reading Festival this summer with me. I can get us both in for nothing. She said she's got some exams that week that she can't miss, and it's out of the question. I said, stuff your exams – you can sit them at a later date. But she won't have it!'

I shook my head too, with what I hoped was manly sympathy. I sucked my drink through a straw, getting the last drops from among the ice cubes. Terry patted me on the back and went to talk with some guys he seemed to know. They greeted him with high-fives, all dressed in those long shorts that hardcore fans wear.

At last the horrible clatter stopped. A few cheers sent the Lancaster lot on their way. Angie stood with her back to the wall, up ahead on my left. As the house DJ put some tunes on, she went into the throng and danced alone. I watched her sway and swirl to some Elbow song about Manchester, with an agony of aches inside me. I was drenched in sadness. My heart felt like someone had torn it out, filled it with concrete, then put it back.

Finally I crept forward, edging through the crush, until I was right behind Angie. Her hair was long and loose. I stood close enough to touch its fragile ends as she slowly danced in a world of her own. My fingers kept brushing the tips of those blue-dyed red-blonde locks. I couldn't take my sad eyes from the white of her neck. Only when the lights dimmed for the main act did we both snap out of our trances.

Seven Seals came on to the crowd all chanting, 'Seee-aaals, Seee-aaaals!' I was kind of hoping they'd suck, so I could get out of my deal with Angie. After all, this was hardly what she'd promised. But the opening number kicked in with two guitars duelling like sword fighters. The lead singer, with his twirly tache, clawed the air like a wild dog. He danced backwards with huge steps, his pointy shoes kicking the air. On some songs he stabbed out cosmic chords on this old keyboard. It was like hearing one of Dad's psychedelic bands crashing the first ever punk party. And they had these choruses that burst over you like flash floods. The whole place was jumping by the end, and the Seals had done south Cumbria proud in the big city.

And then that was it. That was Angie's part of the bargain done with. Now it was down to me to save her from failure at the Wordsworth anniversary event. To admit in public, live on national radio, that I cross-bred daffodils in my private garden. To face a scornful world, who'd wonder why a boy my age couldn't get a real life. That was all I had to look forward to now. That, and the hope of Angie falling for me and my charmless existence. But this looked even more unlikely as I watched her and Terry kiss and make up.

Then Terry came over to me with a cold bottle of Budweiser. He introduced me to the bassist from Seven Seals, who told me about a wild wedding he'd once been to in Millom. We all sat around for ages, talking music like nothing else on the planet mattered more. Some of the other musicians came to join us too, but nobody made me feel left out. They seemed really keen to get the buzz from someone my age. Angie sat on the table's edge and smiled at me sweetly, like a sister. And I smiled back at her, like a brother, through my deep sadness.

TWENTY-SEVEN

It was half past one when we finally left. The house DJ was still knocking out the tunes, but Terry seemed edgy in case Malky was kept waiting.

We motored back through the city, which seemed even more alive and electric than earlier. People out on the town went running across roads right in front of us. We were soon crawling through the murky back streets of Manchester's northern quarter. Terry pulled up at the point where we'd dropped Malky off. It was eerie, dark and quiet. Litter blew along the grey pavement. We were parked by a sex shop with its steel shutters down.

'OK,' said Terry. 'I guess we just sit and wait.'

'What if he doesn't show?' asked Angie.

'He's got my number,' Terry said. 'He'll let us know either way.'

Angie slumped back, knees up. 'You hope,' she said.

Terry turned off the music and we sat in silence. A police car crept across the road just ahead, its light flashing and striping us all in blue. I closed my eyes, though my brain still sang with loud music, and felt warm waves of deep sleep approach. My head was heavy and rolled onto my shoulder. In my first seconds of dreaming, I was resting on Angie's lap. Her fingers were soft across my face—

Thud! Thud! I woke with a gasp. Malky was hammering on the car's roof. Terry wound his window down and handed out a key. Malky snatched it and ran round the back. He threw his rucksack in, and it clunked heavily just like before. If those were building bricks in there, they clearly hadn't been used.

Malky jumped in beside me, muttering dark threats to the world in general.

'OK?' said Terry. 'You ready to—?'

Malky snarled back, 'Just drive!'

Terry started up the engine but it stalled. He tried a few more times, and still the car choked on its own harsh efforts. Malky kicked the back of Terry's seat. He turned to look anxiously through the window behind.

'Get moving!' he shouted. 'Come on, man. Sort it!'

'I'm trying,' said Terry, jumping the ignition again. This time the engine responded and we pulled away with a sudden jolt.

'God shine a light!' said Malky, which seemed a strange thing for a man like him to say. If there *was* a god, then surely he showed himself through things like my daffodils, not by some cranky car starting up to help a criminal. Malky caught me looking sideways at him. His good eye glared back, his wonky one fixed on Angie. I shrank into the corner, clutching the seatbelt.

Terry didn't play any music on the way home. Nobody spoke, either. An air of nervous menace fell over the car, as if we were driving through a war zone and might go straight into a landmine at any second. The motorway flew by in darkness, the lights of distant cities making orange twinkles. The ride was quicker going back, with less traffic around, and Terry stayed in the fast lane most of the way.

Angie's eyes were closed, her head lolling to the right, so I saw her in profile. Headlights from cars behind melted over her face. Her high cheekbones glowed reddy-brown. Her long hair was a nest of hazy shades. Her smooth forehead gleamed with angelic softness. Malky saw me staring at Angie in devotion, and laughed to himself. I closed my eyes and tried to sleep out the journey. I rocked in and out of reality, my mouth wide open as if ready to cry for help.

But Malky wasn't through with me yet. He was going to have his fun with someone, as he'd obviously had a wasted night judging by his mood. As we headed towards Lancaster and the border of south Cumbria, he leaned towards Terry. He grabbed the driver's shoulder and gave it a firm squeeze.

'Let's take the scenic route from here,' he said. 'I fancy the seaside.'

'What's that?' said Terry, hoping Malky was joking. It was already after three a.m.

'I said, let's go and visit the beach. Take the next exit

and get off this damned motorway. I need to feel sea breezes tonight.'

Terry looked at Angie, but she was still crashed out. He glanced in his mirror at me. Our eyes met for a second, but he couldn't have known the surging fear that was quickly making me need a pee. For whatever reason, Malky wanted us to hit the sandy shores of north Lancashire together. Maybe he'd make everyone get out and wander the watery beach in darkness. He knew all about my tragic history with Millom's estuary. Maybe my dad told him once, in all innocence. A little scratch of useless info that could one day be used for Malky's own humour.

Terry turned off at the next junction, and we saw signposts to Hest Bank and Bolton-le-Sands. We were heading for the deepest dangers of Morecambe Bay. I pressed my miserable face to the window, wanting my mum, my dad or my granddad. If this endless night was ever through, I'd take the first bus over to see Granddad whether I'd slept or not.

'Get off this slip road,' said Malky. 'Let's go right back to nature. Have us a little paddle in the sea.'

Soon we were zooming through murky lanes with high hedges. Hardly any other cars were about. Terry looked done in and started yawning. He wound a window down to let the refreshing night air slap him awake. My nose twitched. I could smell salt on the breeze. The sea was close by. We came out at a gloomy crossroads, and Terry swung left down a narrow road. Before long this lane was hugging the coastline. A vast expanse of black sand lay below me, through the window on my left. I felt icy, and buttoned my jacket tightly. Malky lit another of his gruesome cigars. Angie woke up suddenly and looked around in surprise.

Through a long yawn, she asked, 'Where are we?'

'Knocking on for Carnforth,' said Terry, 'on the coast road.'

'Yeah? What we doing out here?'

Terry rolled his eyes quickly, with a slight nod backwards. Angie bit her lower lip.

Malky leaned forward again. 'Somewhere around here,' he said. 'The tide's out. You can drive this useless wreck onto the sands. The fresh air might clean its engine out.'

The road had narrowed to a long lane. Now and then we passed pretty houses by the wayside, with posh cars parked outside. Security lights flared up from garage roofs. And the dark edge of Morecambe Bay was lying in wait to one side.

The lane was lined with clumps of high grasses on our left. These were just a prickly barrier before the strips of sand below. Terry drove slowly through them. Bulrushes and other tall weeds came swishing against my window. The car wobbled along bumpy ground. It chugged across gritty sands that glistened wetly. Small tide pools looked glassy under the moon's light. Terry's car wheels made a slithery sound as they rolled across the bay. Malky urged him to drive further out, then further still.

At last Terry stopped the engine. The night was black and immense, except for the silvery moon. I wished I could fly up to it, on wings made from golden daffodil petals. Nobody spoke in the car for ages. We all sat in dead silence, above the oozing beach.

TWENTY-EIGHT

Malky was the first to move. He got out and took a violent pee on the beach. It sounded like a horse weeing into a tin bucket. Terry glanced in the mirror and saw me clutching my crotch. He knew I wanted to go as well and realized I daren't say so. But the thought of getting out my whatsit anywhere near Angie was making me need to go even more.

'Think I'll join Malky,' said Terry. 'Come on, Andy, let's all be men together.'

I gave him a grateful smile, and got out quickly. I raced over to a clump of sharp rocks that stood like daggers in the shadows. I let out the evening's Coke and bottled beer with a sigh. But suddenly I was aware of sloppy sand under my feet. The old panic attacks kicked in quickly. My shoes felt like they'd found a bed of treacle. For a second I couldn't move or breathe. I stood there rigid, waiting for a certain slow sinking death to follow.

Then I got myself going with a sharp surge of life. Angie was waiting in the car; my granddad was waiting for me in hospital; The Razzler would be waiting for me at home. I looked at the grey-black sky. It was knocking on for daybreak. Sea waves were shushing, like the breathing of a deep-sea monster. The ocean was a murky mirage in the distance.

Back in the car, Malky started going on about the build-up of sand in the Duddon estuary, around Millom. It was like he was trying to freak me out somehow.

'The council in north Lancs are always using dredgers,' he said. 'Great big machines made for cleaning out river beds and stuff. They remove loads of silt and sand from these beaches, to stop it building up. Only then they go and dump it all back into the sea, a couple of miles out. Most of it finds its way into the Duddon. That's why we end up with all that soft sludge around our bay. No wonder people disappear so quickly down it.'

I sat there feeling crushed. *No wonder people disappear so quickly down it.* I had once watched two of them. Angie reached round her seat and tapped my leg in sympathy. I tried reaching down for her fingers, but was just too late.

Terry said, 'OK, then. What do we do now?'

Malky took out what I knew was a joint. He said, 'Why don't we all sit here and have a sweet cigarette?'

Terry risked a glance at his watch, but no hint was taken behind him. 'Just a quick one,' he dared to say. 'Gotta drive these guys home safely.'

I knew he was dying to get Angie back to his pad in Ulverston. You could hardly blame him, but I just wanted to be off the beach. The longer we stayed, and the more Malky got stoned, the bigger the chance he'd make something nasty happen. I took deep and quiet breaths, staring back towards the comfort of that road beyond. The tall grasses there made a thick barricade, as if to trap me on the dark sands for ever.

Malky smiled grimly. 'I hope your mother's not waiting up, Angela,' he said. It was the first time he'd spoken to her all night. Angie didn't answer, but reached for the pile of CDs under her seat. She rifled through them and picked out some Pink Floyd.

Dreamy and haunting waves of music washed around the car from speaker to speaker. The small space inside soon filled with smoke too, a rich and earthy smoke that made me think of dark soil after rainfall. I couldn't help but inhale it. Angie took a drag on Malky's big spliff, then passed it to me. I was terrified of the stuff, and shook my head.

Just then, the moon slid behind stormy clouds, and the night around us grew intense. We'd been out on the beach for fifteen minutes now. That was the longest I'd spent on any sands for over six years. I sank into the corner against the door, biting my hand to stop the hysterical terror escaping.

The other three were getting high. Terry began to smile and his shoulders shook lightly. Angie was rocking back and forth beside him. Even Malky's face lost its craggy grimness. He chuckled to himself like some old wino. All the time, Pink Floyd caressed the car with softly strange melodies and voices that seemed to vibrate in the mind like you were under hypnosis. I felt a bit calmer, now that everyone was more chilled. Angie put a hand over the back of her seat. As Malky and Terry both had their eyes closed, I softly let my right hand steal out to stroke hers. She nabbed one of my fingers and gave it a quick squeeze. I sat back with a heart-heavy sigh.

I closed my eyes too, hoping that sleep would take me and I'd awake as the sun began to rise over Millom. I was off in seconds, and in my dreams I was walking along the river Duddon with Granddad, and all our daffodils there had petals of pure gold. A cloud of yellow pollen blew about like magic dust. The day was brilliant and blue, with bees buzzing from flower to flower in search of sweetness. And my granddad was so strong and alive just then. He was talking to me, his head of silvery hair all shiny. I couldn't hear what he was saying, but it seemed important.

I awoke suddenly, with a parched mouth and a stale scent in my nose. I was dying for some fresh air after my dreams of open country. My eyes were dry and tired. I felt a crush of despair that the car hadn't moved anywhere. No mountains beckoning from the motorway as we cruised back into the Cumbrian dawn.

The car wobbled, in what I thought was the strong night breeze that had risen. Malky was asleep, the fag end of his joint in one hand. Terry and Angie were also dozing, their knees touching and hands locked. I grunted with despair. The dreamy dregs of Pink Floyd's CD were fading. Also dying out were the sky's dismal clouds, which were now threatened by a lighter backdrop. But a ghostly gloom still hung around, as if some storm cloud had been lowered to protect us.

The car lurched again like it was tired of sitting there, and wanted to head home. I stared over at the banks of weeds and grasses to my left, lining the road away from there. I frowned, and thought they couldn't be the same wild plants as before. They looked even taller than earlier. The car took another judder.

I peered over towards the narrow lane. And that's when I sat up in real shock. I pressed my hands to the glass like a prisoner. The rows of tall grasses had grown again. They had, they really *had* shot up further in a few seconds. I now couldn't see their tops from where I sat. Before I'd fallen asleep, their whole height had been visible.

I scrambled to open the window, with hands that I'd lost control of. It unwound stiffly with heavy creaks. I jammed my head and shoulders through, then pushed my top half right out. As I overbalanced, my face nearly hit the sand below. All my breath got squeezed into a tight fist. I opened my mouth wide. Finally . . . *finally*, I let out a scream of terror.

I fell back into the car, shoving Malky, slapping Angie, yelling at Terry.

'The car's going down!' I cried. 'Get up, get up! *We're sinking!*'

They awoke slowly. I punched them all again, hearing their sleepy protests. Malky lashed out in reflex, and caught my forehead with a ringed finger.

Angie shouted, 'What's happening?' But Terry had realized already, and sprawled across to open her window.

'Throw yourself out!' he yelled. '*Do it! Do it!*'

'Terry!' screamed Angie. She didn't understand.

I shouted in her ear. 'We're on quicksand! The car's going under. Get out and go flat on your belly. Crawl away quickly!'

Still she didn't move. For a second I thought her weak and silly.

'*Come on!*' I cried out. Then I thought of how I was once a weak and silly boy. The yellow-orange shirt of that young lad and his father's brown jacket flooded my vision. I saw them sink under, still straining for life.

But I wouldn't just sit there awaiting my fate. I'd been planning for this moment ever since I saw those two tourists drowning. Over and over in my mind, every possible setting, every angle and escape.

Terry and Malky got their windows down, the doors being wedged in sludge. They both went headfirst into the chilly dawn. I heard a slap as they landed wetly. And that's when Angie turned to me, her face a mask of terror.

'Andrew!' she begged. 'Help me!' She reached out her hands and grabbed my head. For a second, our faces were so close I thought we might kiss. But the agony on her pale face fired me up. I tugged her window down, then my own. By now, Terry and Malky were crawling to safety. They'd saved themselves first.

I was making a wild guess here that we'd survive. If the sands had taken this long to suck down a hefty car, then they'd support a human's weight for long enough to escape. I lifted Angie by the arm and got her to the window.

That's when she squealed, shook me away and sank back into her seat.

'I can't!' she wailed. 'I just can't!'

TWENTY-NINE

'Listen!' I shouted. My voice seemed to echo for miles through the stillness. I held Angie's shoulders.

'I'll be right beside you,' I urged her. 'Shove yourself through and land flat. Then crawl quickly, and I *mean* quickly, until the beach feels firmer. Then you stand and walk away. Got it? I won't leave you.'

She nodded and sobbed, tossing aside her wild hair. 'Promise?' she said.

My heart was bulging with emotion. 'I'll never leave you,' I whispered.

I hung back out of the car window, and waited till Angie was in the same position.

'Ready?' I said. 'Just do it. *Now!*'

We both tumbled out as the car took another lunge down. Its wheels were way below. As I'd thought, the quicksand was fairly weak. It needed the incoming tide to soften it more for lethal intent.

We landed with two matching splats. I made Angie get moving right away. We were both slimed with grots of sand. I inched over to her as we struggled across the sloppy beach.

'Onto your hands and knees!' I ordered. She followed

my lead, and we crawled like giant crabs further to safety. I felt the bubbling and sucking right under my body. Even then I knew if I'd slept another ten minutes, it would have been too late. The tide, the 'galloping horse', was racing in. I could hear the urgent boom of its hooves, growing nearer, growing louder.

At last I felt a tougher grittiness in the sand. 'Stand up,' I told Angie. 'Then take big steps, landing lightly. Don't hang about in between. Get going.'

We both strode forward like two kids playing a strange beach game. When the ground seemed much firmer, I stopped and held Angie's arm to steady her. That's when I glanced behind for a second. Malky and Terry were still round the other side of the sinking car, wrestling on the sands. They were on a sloppy patch, in great danger. Malky's hands were on Terry's neck. Terry shook him off as Malky slid forward to try and reach the doomed vehicle.

'You're mad!' shouted Terry. 'Just leave it, man. It's only a rucksack!' He ran away, in a wide arc, slipping and splashing towards us.

Malky ignored him and trod into the slushy beach. He was almost wading, with clumsy steps that nearly brought him to his knees. Those cowboy boots were no match for Morecambe Bay's demons. And by now, Terry's car was mostly heading under. Its open windows let oozes of gunk flow inside. Its faded paintwork gave a last gasp. The sand sucked and slurped, as if enjoying such a great conquest. The car's red roof left a dark glow. For a second I saw the moon reflected upon it.

'Keep going,' I told Angie. 'Head for those long grasses.' But she wouldn't leave her lover, who had left her to me only minutes ago.

'Terry!' she cried out. 'Terry, what's going on?'

Malky was still trying to slip through sludge and reach the car. Terry tried shouting him back again. Only when Malky felt the pull of a hollow below did he clamber away from the dying vehicle. His cross-eyes were wide with anger. I thought maybe the devil's own sockets could glare like that.

He stood staring after Terry's lost car. He sank to his knees, head arched back to the heavens. His tight white trousers, lined with purple sequins, were filthy. His boots were coated with muck. Even his fancy overcoat had splatters all over it. Terry edged away towards me and Angie at the back of the beach. Angie ran over to him, which nearly made me throw up. She flung her arms around his neck as he patted her back.

And that's the last thing I knew just then. The sheer shock of those last minutes did me in. My brain failed where my body had fought so hard. Black shadows were flapping around me like a swarm of bats. The terror of my ordeal came screaming into my veins like a burning poison.

I recall a sense of falling over a cliff and landing miles

away. In truth, I just passed out and fell back into the massed grasses. I never felt a thing.

As my eyes flickered, I heard Angie's anxious voice. 'Andrew! Andy!' she cried. I felt light slaps to my face. 'Are you OK? Can you hear me?'

I began to come round, but kept my eyes closed in the hope that Angie might try some kiss-of-life thingy. All I felt was Malky's muddy cowboy boot under my bum. He tried to kick me up with it.

'Leave him,' said Angie crossly. 'He's only a boy.'

That annoyed me. In the dark depths of my fainting fit, I could still get upset. Surely I had just proved to Angie that I was more than a boy. I hadn't noticed the main man Terry stick around when disaster struck.

I sat up slowly, Angie's arms around my shoulders. I rested my head there, and she kissed my brown hair. I hadn't known such comfort in years, and began to cry quietly. The strain of that whole mad night was kicking in. Angie cradled me.

'When you wet tossers are quite ready,' said Malky, 'we've got a new motor to snatch from somewhere. Get off your knees, kids. Move it.'

We all got busy at Malky's command. Like a bunch of shipwreck survivors, we straggled away from the beach towards the road above. Malky stormed off ahead, and we followed him as if too scared to disobey our leader. Terry tried to comfort Angie, but she wouldn't walk beside him now, and instead walked almost in my shadow. I still felt bushed, after passing out and landing with a hard crunch. The back of my head was numb.

Cold and sludgy, we trudged along the narrow road. Woodlands rose up on our right, and the dark bay was down to our left. The lane seemed to drag on for ever, without any sign of human life, until we reached a small hotel. It had whitewashed walls, big bay windows and a few cars parked outside. Malky went up to each vehicle in turn, peering through the windscreens or fiddling with handles. At last he chose a red Fiat and took out something from his big coat.

I closed my eyes, swaying slightly, as Malky fiddled and swore. Then I heard him say, 'Gotcha!' Malky got in and started messing around among the control panels. We all stood outside, in a light drizzle, as if waiting to be invited on board. The car's motor went *a-ra-ra-ra-ra-rah* and its headlights came on. Malky quickly jumped out. 'You drive,' he said to Terry. 'The less of my prints left around the better. Be quick.'

Terry got in the front with Angie beside him. Me and Malky were stuck with each other in the back again. We all belted up except Malky, who clearly thought he was immortal. Terry pulled away from the hotel as quietly as he could, though I saw a curtain twitch upstairs as we left. I ducked out of sight.

'Crack on,' ordered Malky. 'Foot down hard.'

Soon we were zapping back along the main roads, which were busier now with heavy lorries. Daylight lifted the sombre gloom of this dragging night. The gears grunted and slid as Terry got used to a strange motor. Malky's hands and knees were twitching and drumming, like he couldn't bear to stay still. Angie sat with her head to the window, staring sadly out at nothing.

We skirted the peninsula where the river Kent flows in from the sea and heads north to Kendal. Then it was up towards Newby Bridge, at the south end of Lake Windermere. The dual carriageway was wet with rainfall. Heavy lorries thundered along it, their wheels spurting sprays of water. The light showers of earlier had turned heavier. Our windscreen wipers scraped across, and the car was miserably cold inside. But at least we were back among familiar landscapes. Green-brown hills were misting over in the background.

'Get off the main drag,' said Malky. 'We might have been reported.'

Terry drove like someone on automatic, and soon we were making for comforting little villages like Lowick. Soaking sheep were grazing on dewy pastures, or huddling against dry-stone walls.

Malky had a call on his mobile. He listened hard for a second, then clicked off without reply. He leaned forward again. 'Drop me in Barrow,' he said to Terry. 'I've a bit of business there to take care of.'

Terry tried to sound jokey. 'You're kidding, man,' he

said. 'That's gonna add another two hours on for these guys. And this thing's running low on gas.'

'Just do it,' said Malky.

Terry sighed as loud as he dared. But I was almost pleased. My granddad was probably dying in Barrow hospital, not far from where we were now heading. He wanted to see me before he went away to the sunless land. And I wanted to say again that I forgave him for not being there on that fateful Sunday afternoon six years earlier. Terry did a violent U-turn on a narrow lane, and we surged back towards the heavier traffic.

Then came that scary stretch of the A590. We were on the notorious road of doom. There's a big warning sign up on either side of this route. It lets you know how many deaths or serious accidents there have been along it that year. It's roughly one every day. Someone must be up there painting a new figure on it all the time. Maybe they could just install a kind of scoreboard thing, and operate it by hand.

As you head into Ulverston, from where we picked up the A590 near Haverthwaite, things turn pretty hairy. It's like getting on a roller coaster that you know has collapsed the year before. I checked my seatbelt, and checked Angie's too. Malky tutted, as if he despaired of such feeble concerns. He cracked his knuckles, making my stomach heave.

Terry picked up speed, looking well hacked off. Whatever plans he'd been making for him and Angie were now done for. A dull slog to Barrow and back lay ahead, with every chance of a police alert over the car we'd nicked.

Traffic on the dual carriageway suddenly slowed. Both lanes were full. A tractor had joined the line of vehicles in our lane, just up ahead. Its farmer driver cared nothing for the dull pace we were all forced to endure behind him. He sat plumply on a plastic seat, chugging along.

'Come on, come *on*,' urged Terry.

'Flatten the fat prat,' said Malky.

There was a major intersection looming, turning right to the tiny hamlet of Greenodd. The tractor spurted off towards Greenodd, and the wild landscapes beyond there for Coniston. As it left us, everyone picked up their pace with a vengeance. There was a great roar of dust and diesel, with Terry joining in and putting his foot right down. The lorry in front spurted vile smoke at us. Our windscreen was drenched in spray from its back wheels.

Way up on our right stood another small village, hidden behind towering pine trees. It's a place so trivial that many maps don't include it. But it does have a track sloping down through the trees, which suddenly joins the main road. And at that point, the dual carriageway narrows to a single lane.

There were roadworks up ahead. Even this early, the sound of heavy drilling was adding to the thud of cars and lorries. I was drifting off again, seeing quicksand behind closed eyes, wanting Angie in my arms. It was an effort to stay awake, with my head lolling, so I missed some of what happened next.

Terry hit the brakes with real force. I slammed forward, my seatbelt snapping into safety mode. Everything was a flash of violent colours. The dark blue of a car alongside. The grimy white of the lorry in front. The bright yellow of a van speeding down that side road.

Then we were shoved from behind. It was like a game of pinball. We were the silver ball being bullied from side to side. We hit the bumpers of that truck in front. The van flicked us sideways. We skidded and swerved. Then something pounded us with real force from what felt like every direction. Terry lost control, his feet slipping across the pedals. We revved up, then rolled. Somewhere down to my left, a muddy river bed blinked back. A wide wetland was ready to catch us.

Next thing, we crashed through some fencing on the roadside. The world went upside down. The roller coaster had crumbled. Angie screamed. Terry slapped at the steering wheel. The dirty waterway just outside Ulverston lay waiting. We hurtled towards sandy swamps, where cows and sheep often met their drowned fate.

A thundering head hit my face. Malky had been thrown across the car. His forehead struck me like an iron ingot. In a blitz of blinding stars I tried to scream blue murder. A molten fist had been buried in my right cheek.

I was inside the old mining furnace of Millom, my head boiling into oblivion. Then it was being pounded out of shape. I fell through the darkness, melting away to nothing, sweating with agony.

THIRTY

Someone was trying to force my eyes open. I wished they wouldn't, as it awoke me to the evil pains in my head. A bright light shone into my pupils. I tried to blink against the fingers that held my lids.

'This one's with us too,' said a man's voice. His breath was minty. I got a glimpse of a yellow jacket. Now the throbbings around my face were too strong for me to stay knocked out. I opened both eyes and saw the other passengers outside. Terry was on a stretcher; Angie was being given first aid; and Malky was using his rotten mobile. He strutted around on the edge of the boggy creek, with hardly a scratch on him. Maybe he had nine lives, like some devilish cat.

They put me on a stretcher. Angie's forehead was cut and she was crying. As I was carried up the grassy bank to an ambulance, she hobbled after me. I flung out a hand towards her, like I'd floated into some tragic movie scene.

'You OK?' she sniffled, grasping my fingers.

I could hardly speak for all my agony. 'Yeah,' I coughed. 'You?'

She nodded. 'Terry's in a bad way,' she said. 'I'll see you at the hospital.'

I think they gave me morphine, or such like. I passed out again, and the next thing I knew was a bright hospital ward. Barrow Infirmary. I felt terribly sick, and something huge had grown on my face like a tumour. The nurses washed me, soothed me, bandaged me and got some hot soup down my dry throat. I'd no idea what time it was, but I knew it was still Saturday. And then my mum turned up, and she'd brought Abayakurti along too with his baldy blessings and sex magic.

Mum flung herself onto the bed. She gripped my hand, speaking almost crazily, her eyes already blurred with tears. 'What ... What's going on ...? Why are you ...? Where have you ...? What's been ...?'

It hurt to speak, and I sounded like a northern robot. 'Car accident,' I said, through my teeth. 'Went to a gig in Manchester. Got back a bit late.'

Mum's eyes were wild and confused. She looked so small sitting there, with short black hair, her nose and lips pierced. 'Yes, but ... the car ... they said ... was it *stolen*?'

I slowly nodded. 'A long story,' I gurgled. 'Another time.'

Mum nodded. Abayakurti's eyes were closed, his lips muttering in prayer. Mum said, 'We can't get hold of your dad. Any idea where he might be?'

A slow headshake. Then I tried to sit upright, with a sudden thought. 'How's Granddad?' I managed to gurgle. 'Is he nearby?'

Mum looked behind her to where a nurse was barging

into the ward. 'He's in a different wing of the hospital,' she said. 'Don't worry about Granddad right now. He's safe enough.'

I slumped slowly back. 'How's Terry?' I asked. 'Have they said?'

'Who? Oh, the driver. Not good, though he's not dead or anything. And what on *earth* was Malcolm Dowder doing with you?'

I offered another slow headshake, and a few spilling tears. I was trembling back to the quicksand scare, saving my angel Angie again, feeling her warm caress afterwards, and reliving the car hurtling downhill to its doom. Abayakurti made a steeple of his hands, then laid them on my scalp. 'We should leave Andrew to the medical staff,' he said. 'We will come back later and bring some healing creams. You will be fine with proper rest and proper care.'

He left without blessing me, although I wouldn't have minded this time. In the bed beside me, some old bloke was just out of surgery after a knee operation. He called for a drink so often, and so loudly, that I almost got out of bed and threw my own jug of water over him. Then finally The Razzler turned up, his mohican looking more normal without any dye. His hair was even growing again around the sides that he normally shaved. I thought he might joke about my mad night of rock 'n' roll excess. But he looked angry, and he sounded it.

'It's not just you I'm mad at,' he said. 'It's myself

mostly. Mad at the mess I've made of looking after you. Mad at the rotten example I must have been setting. But what the hell made you go off to Manchester, staying out all night with some radio DJ and a small-town crook? Hmm? And I've had Ma Hutchinson going berserk in my ear about Angie. I can't see her putting this in her local news column.'

Through throaty croaks, and with a swollen tongue, I told Dad all I could manage. He still looked hacked off, but calmed down a bit near the end. I wanted to ask about his illness, about that cancer book and his new diet. In the end, all I said was, 'Where were you today? No one could find you.'

He avoided my eyes. 'I was . . . in a meeting some-where. Nothing vital. But as for you right now, the doctor says they can discharge you after the weekend. No school for a while. Do you want to stay with me or your mum?'

'Don't mind,' I said.

'Right, well, come back to Millom first. That's where all your things are. Oh, and Angie sends her love to you. She escaped with just heavy bruises. Now she's gone home with Ma Hutch, and heck knows what's being said there right now. Poor kid. No wonder she always wanted to cut loose, with such a stiff old stick for a mother.'

After he left me I passed out with tiredness and painkillers. But I awoke not much later, and stared at the hospital floor in horror. It had become a sludgy pit of brown and black. A wet bog of quicksand. And my bed was sinking quickly, just like Terry's car had earlier. I tried to climb out of it, screaming and shouting, until two nurses came flying in to inject me with something.

Even then, I dreamed of golden beaches that cracked open like earthquakes. I awoke in tears, knowing this coastline's curse would never leave me now.

THIRTY-ONE

They let me go on Sunday evening, to zoom away with Dad in his red sports car. I asked if I could visit Granddad before we left, but Dad said they were keeping him quiet just for now.

He got me settled on the sofa at home, wrapped in a duvet, with a bowl of home-made cabbage broth. He sat down in the armchair to my left, his sad eyes fixed on me.

My swollen face had gone down a bit, and speaking was easier. 'Dad,' I said, 'I need to know something. Don't be mad with me. But I found that book on cancer under the sofa. The one you tried to hide. And the leaflet about Gerson therapy inside it. What's with all these big changes you're making?'

Dad stood up and went to the drawn curtains. Then he turned to face me, eyes downcast behind those tinted brown glasses. 'Yes,' he said. 'There's something wrong. I've got a little lump somewhere, that shouldn't exist. I've had tests and there's evidence of some cancerous cells. Your mum once told me about this Gerson therapy. It's a way of healing yourself with natural goodness. You bombard the body with organic juices and healthy foods. I figured anything was better than all that chemo stuff, where your hair falls out and you turn into a living wreck.'

I felt cold all over and hugged the duvet. 'I saw a benefit cheque arrive last week,' I said. 'But that can't be paying for all this posh food. Organic stuff costs a fortune.'

Dad nodded, hands behind his back. He looked me squarely in the eyes. 'There was some money left by your Grandma Hebthwaite,' he said. 'She was pretty savvy with stocks and shares for such a quiet woman. That's how your granddad could afford to be kept in that nice care home. She left most of it to him and your mother. But there was another lot she handed down too.'

I sat up in surprise. 'You don't mean she left it to *you*,' I said. 'She didn't approve of you marrying Mum, did she?'

'No, she never cared much for me,' Dad said. 'And it was *you* she left the money to, Andy. It wasn't for me. It's for when you turn eighteen, but it was placed in my account for safekeeping. I'm afraid I've been spending your inheritance. It's the way I've chosen to try and keep myself alive. But I'll pay it all back when I'm better. And I will be better. In time.'

I didn't care about the money, and told my dad so right then. I just wanted him to stick around in my life. To be there through the highs and lows yet to come. We faced each other with tearful eyes. The soft glow of Dad's reading lamp was yellow like a daffodil. The street outside was quiet for once, as if respecting this big moment. There was one more thing I had to ask.

'Dad,' I said, 'where is it, this . . . lump? I mean, is it something they can easily operate on? Or is it buried somewhere inside, where it's more tricky?'

That's when Dad's face began to frown with pain. His forehead creased into thick worry lines. With a shaky hand, he very slowly pointed a path down his body. He kept going, until he'd reached below his middle. Then his finger curved inward, and aimed at his private parts. His trembling hand finally stopped its journey just by his trouser zip. My dad's face was red with stress. He shook his head in dismay or disbelief.

I bit a thumbnail with rapid nibbles. 'Can they . . . Can they cure it?' I asked quietly.

Dad was nodding very slightly. 'I really hope so,' he whispered. 'I think we found it in time.'

I breathed out heavily. 'Yeah,' I said. 'I know you'll be OK, Razzle. You always make things turn out right.'

I thought that might be the hardest conversation of my life. But there was another one to follow that night, just as difficult in its own way. Mum came over from Ulverston in her cranky old car. Even when I heard it splutter to a halt outside, at ten o'clock, I thought nothing was too wrong. Just a quick check-up on the naughty patient.

Dad left us alone in the living room, still lit by just that one lamp. Mum stroked my hair, rubbed arnica cream on my bruised face and kissed my brow. She sat on the sofa where I lay all wrapped in the duvet. We made small talk about the accident, how very silly I had been, how lucky I was, and how much she'd been worried. I nodded and sighed and ached along with Mum's words.

'How's Granddad?' I asked, when I could finally get a word in.

Mum reached over to grip my hand and closed her eyes. Her fingers squeezed mine tightly. I squeezed back.

'Mum?' I said, going all shivery. 'Has he got much worse?'

At last she whispered to me, like it was our special secret. Like nobody else on earth would ever need to know.

'He's dead, Andy. Your granddad has passed away. That's really what I came over to tell you.'

I let go her hand and sat up with a shout. 'He's not dead! He wants to see me. I'm going over to see him. That's what we arranged!'

Mum nodded, trying to grasp my hot hand again. I shrank away from her into the corner of the sofa. I turned my head and buried my face among cushions and pillows.

'I know, I know,' she said. 'He was waiting for you. But by the end I don't think he even realized that I was there with him. He slipped away quietly in the morning, just before you were brought to the hospital. That's how I happened to be there when you arrived. I couldn't tell you at the time, as you were still in shock after the accident.'

I let out a terrible wail of protest. I had been so close to my granddad at the end, and yet nowhere near him.

Dad came running in when he heard my howl. 'Have you told him?' he asked.

Mum gave him a hopeless look and sighed. 'Obviously,' she said. Dad just nodded, and slunk back to the kitchen like a dog in disgrace. When my tears finally dried up, I let Mum hold me against her.

She said, 'You were always more than just his grandson. He was my father, and you're my only child. That made you extra special for him. And he was so happy when you inherited his love of daffodils, and all that talent you have with flowers.'

I rubbed my eyes, pushing back the floods behind them. 'Did he say anything at the end?' I said. 'Did he mention me?'

Through a shiny blur I saw Mum smiling. 'Of course,' she said. 'He asked me to tell you something. He said you must always be true to those you love. He also said you must leave the past behind now, and to forgive yourself as you have forgiven others. I'm sure that's what he said. Does it make sense?'

I nodded. 'I think so,' I said. 'I think I know what he meant.'

That made Mum happy. 'And now, just bear with me,' she said. 'Hear me out with what else I need to say.' She smoothed damp hair from my face, and looked closely at me.

'You were asking about Skyros recently,' she said. 'And after what's been happening to you here, I've now made up my mind. Skyros is a beautiful place, an island where people with my sort of skills can go to teach, and learn. Being stuck in a small town like Millom isn't doing you any good, Andy. So after this summer, when your exams are done, I want you to come away to Skyros with me. To experience a new life, a whole new *way* of life, and to heal all the unhappiness you've ever known.'

I stared at Mum, not really understanding. 'But I've always lived *here*,' I said. 'When would we come back? How long are you going for?'

Mum held my face between her hands. 'I'm getting out for good,' she said. 'I'm not coming back. It's time for a new start somewhere safe and warm, away from all this cold and drizzle. And I want you to come with me. To explore a new and higher culture. Abayakurti will also join us for some of the time.'

I shook my head, my mind spinning. 'But . . . I mean, how would we live?'

Mum told me how she could run classes in the summer schools on Skyros. And we could spend the rest of our time travelling and exploring. I'd be free to return home if I didn't like it, or wanted a change. But all I could think of then was Angie, and my daffodils, and who on earth would look out for The Razzler. Mum sat there looking hopeful as I chewed my lips in slow thought.

'It sounds like you've got it all decided,' I said. 'The only thing is, before you make any more plans, I think there's something big you should know. It's about my dad.'

THIRTY-TWO

It was nearly a week before I faced the world again. I grieved for Granddad and spent many hours in my private garden, hidden from everything.

On the Friday of Granddad's funeral, I walked behind the coffin holding a bunch of his Golden Glories. The morning was bright, making me feel warmed like an open fire. And the sun seemed to burn in the very heart of those daffodils that I carried.

Granddad was buried not far from the grave of Mrs Tyson's husband. My flowery heart of Mystics all stood bowing gently, as if paying their due respects. People looked at my secretly planted work with admiring eyes, after Granddad was laid to rest nearby. But there was no gesture big enough I could offer to him. No tree-pattern, no heart-shape, no mass of daffs covering the wide world with glory.

Instead, I waited for the guests and mourners to toddle off to the wake in the church hall. From my jacket pocket I took out a single bulb. It was the size and shape of a small onion. With bare hands, I dug into freshly turned soil on the grave.

I would plant just one daffodil there, right over where

I thought Granddad's heart must be. The name of this variety was April Tears. From early March in the following year it would be in full bloom. I dug a small hole down with the scutcher, to insert an April Tears bulb.

My fingers got grubby, and my nails filled with earth. I heard footsteps behind and thought Mum had come back. I never knew what passed between her and Dad on the night I told her of his illness, but she'd been to visit him three times since. Dismayed by his news, but happy with his response, she was helping The Razzler's recovery.

It wasn't my mum behind me. It was Angie. No trace of that blue hair dye now. It was back to her normal strawberry-blonde crowning glory. She wore a lacy white top and creamy trousers. It was like an angel, a blissful soul, had come down to watch over Granddad. She hovered shyly at a distance. I waved her over.

She knelt beside me on the grass. 'Hiya,' she said nervously. 'How've you been?'

I packed the soil tightly over that April Tears bulb. 'My head still feels a bit whacked,' I said. 'Otherwise OK. I heard Terry got allowed home.'

'Mmm. Yeah, he's out, though I won't be seeing him again. The police paid him a little visit. Didn't he know I was only a sixth-form girl? they asked. Terry sent me a pretty horrible text about it. I can't blame him.'

'No,' I said, stroking the earth. 'No, you can't really.'

Angie nodded. 'At least Terry got a new car out of it.

Malky bought him one, to shut him up about that night when his old one sank. But the police pulled Terry in for questioning when he left hospital. I hope they don't pin anything too serious on him.'

I shook my head. 'He'll be OK,' I said. 'But I hope they send Malky down.'

Angie sat back, brushing her trousers. She said, 'I'm so sorry for everything.' Her voice got choky; she put her head on her knees. 'I wish I could take it all back. And you were so brave.'

I stroked a strand of that heavenly hair. 'It's OK,' I said softly. 'And I'll still help you with that Wordsworth poem thingy. I'm gonna do it for my granddad too.'

Angie's head nodded against her knees. She sniffed and rubbed her blue eyes. Yes, they really were blue, the first time I'd noticed. The colour of the spring sky, or of the sea when it breaks against The Blocks on Millom beach. 'Thank you,' she said. 'You been back to school yet?'

'No,' I said. 'You?'

Angie shook her head. 'Guess we'll both have to face the music together,' she said.

'Guess we will,' I said. I stood slowly, reaching for Angie's hand to haul her up. 'I bet the local gossips have had a field day over us.'

Angie gave a sad smile. 'Then we'll have to give them something real to talk about,' she said. 'Won't we, Mr Flower Power?'

* * *

And so the following Monday morning Angie and I stood in the headmistress's office like scolded puppies. Mrs Longden's eyes glowed like two white rocks on The Slaggy. I felt them burning for hours after.

'Although this wasn't a school matter,' she said, 'I am not pleased at having the police calling by. What you do with your lives beyond school is your business, but your actions – and the actions of others involved – do not reflect well on us here.'

'Yes, Mrs Longden,' said Angie.

'No, Mrs Longden,' I said at the same time. I fought back a giggle.

'Yes, no, whatever,' said the headmistress. 'In a week's time the BBC broadcast will offer you two a chance for redemption. I understand, Andrew, that you have a certain gift with daffodils. Some sort of cross-breeding is involved. Is that correct?'

I nodded.

'Well, between your two talents the event should be memorable. And you *will* both make it memorable and a credit to the town and the school. Am I getting through?'

'Yes, Mrs Longden,' we said together.

'I very much hope so. I will be attending your rehearsal at lunch time, Angela. I hope that I like what I see and hear. As for you, Andrew, I would like to read some notes of what you plan to broadcast. You may both go.'

'Thank you, Mrs Longden,' we said.

So we emerged back into the glare of school life, expecting nudges and stares at every corner. In fact, we got gazes of admiration and looks of awe. Everyone turned and stared after us in the corridors, or shouted wild words of support. It seemed that a rock-'n'-roll road trip to Manchester, ending in near disaster, worked wonders for your reputation. I forgot all about my FA Cup ears and strutted around like a hero.

I went with Angie up to the library later, where loads more kids had signed up for her poetry reading in Hawkshead. We stared at the poster in amazement. I bashed out some basic notes about petals, stamens, pollen and seed pods for Mrs Longden.

And then, about half an hour before afternoon school, we went to the sports hall. Here was more proof that me and Angie had achieved a new status over the past week. There were so many people gathered inside that I had to dash upstairs and photocopy extra sheets of 'Daffodils'. When Angie called for hush, the place fell quiet within seconds. The wild rock goddess had their full attention now. Even the dumb drongos at the back held their poems at the ready.

Angie was well fired up by the time Mrs Longden sneaked in. 'Right!' she shouted. 'You all have the words at hand. By the time this is broadcast, live on BBC Radio Four, you must know them off by heart. Anyone who needs a crib sheet on the day can stand outside and not take part!'

Angie stopped and cleared her white throat. I gazed at her, and thought back to the quicksand terror. All I needed to remember was how she'd cradled me afterwards.

'OK, let's have a run through,' she shouted. 'Stay in time with me, watch for my signals, and for pity's sake . . . just read the words like they actually *mean* something!'

And so we began. But this time there were no murky mumblings. This time it sounded like we were all chanting away with William Wordsworth, two hundred years ago on the banks of Ullswater, where he was first inspired to write his poetic lullaby.

> *'I wandered lonely as a Cloud . . .*
> *That floats on high o'er Vales and Hills . . .'*

THIRTY-THREE

One night that week, in the early hours, the police raided Millom's main nightclub. It stood in the town square, near some new holiday flats that were being sold off for massive sums. The club itself was called Reflections, but it was known as Rejections on account of the losers who partied there.

Malky was known to have a big hand in running the place. Probably used it as a selling point for his rotten drugs. It was my dad who told me what happened as I got ready for school. I sat at the kitchen table, eating organic granola with yoghurt and strawberries. Well, it was me paying for all this stuff, so why not enjoy it? My eyes were glued to a copy of Wordsworth's 'Daffodils' as I went over it one more time.

The Razzler had already lost weight, his eyes were brighter and his face looked years younger.

'There's a load of police down from Carlisle,' he said. 'They're not in anyone's pay, or taking bribes from local insiders. They've been pulling people in to question them. I'd expect one or two to crack under pressure.'

'About time,' I said. 'What are they searching for?'

Dad laughed, and scraped out the juicer. The scraggy

flesh and blood of strawberries dripped into a jug. 'Gold!'
he said. 'They're searching for pure gold! It seems that
Malky had a cosy little sideline going. He's been melting
down a load of stolen jewellery and pouring the precious
stuff into moulds. Those old ingot moulds they once used
down the iron mines.'

I was only half listening, absorbed as I was in
Wordsworth. But something in what my dad said made
me sit up.

'Ingot moulds?' I said. 'Didn't Malky ask you to make
some for him?'

'Aye, he did. But my dealings with him are long done.
They've raided his gloomy old mansion above the bay,
and even taken away his gunsights to examine.'

I put Wordsworth aside. 'Go back a bit,' I said. 'You
mean the police haven't found these gold ingots yet, or
whatever they are?'

'Nope,' Dad said, slurping strawberry smoothie. His
mouth was ringed with red froth. 'That's why they're
turning over half the town and village. Looks like Malky
learned a few tricks from the old mining industry. All the
police found was a cast-iron smelting pot standing on
breeze blocks in his outside building. He must have used
it for heating up the jewellery that those desperate
druggies exchanged.'

Even I laughed at this. 'Just like Granddad always
told me,' I said. 'Skim off the scum and you'll find
precious nuggets below. Malky knew it too.'

'True enough,' said Dad. 'Malky was carrying on the great Millom tradition of smelting and skimming. Years ago, they poured hot metal into moulds for iron, and now it's dodgy gold. But without the actual ingots, the police have no evidence. Malky must be sitting on a small fortune. I wonder where he's hiding them.'

I finished my breakfast and left Dad to his meditation. He'd been going over to Conishead Priory early most mornings to reflect with the Buddhists, which is why he'd gone missing on the morning of my accident. It's also why I saw him driving there on the day of that school trip to Barrow.

'See you tonight,' I said. 'Oh, and I just might be late back from school.'

Angie cornered me at break. Rays of spring sunshine glowed upon her like cathedral light. I thought of her captured in stained glass.

'Oh, my life!' she gushed. 'Oh . . . my . . . *life!*'

'You sound pleased,' I said. 'What's new?'

She was all fidgets and fuss. 'You'll just *never* guess who's gonna be in Hawkshead, at Wordsworth's old school, on the day of our event there!'

My mind raced. The Prime Minister? England's football manager? Johnny Depp?

Angie didn't wait for me to think further. She rattled off the name of some bloke, stressing his first and last names, her eyes wide. I'd never heard of this guy. Angie can't have noticed my dumb look.

She said, 'He only, like, won the Legacy Prize for poetry last year. He's doing a reading at Dove Cottage on the night of our event, but he's coming over to take part in the BBC broadcast in the morning. Amazing!'

She handed me a copy of this poet's book. Turning it over, I found his photo. Yep, that figured. He was about thirty, windswept black hair, darkly intelligent eyes. No hint of FA Cup ears or puppy-fat cheeks. If he dared steal my thunder on the day . . .

Angie jigged about. 'I'll have to show him some of my own stuff,' she said. 'You never know – this time next year I could be a published poet too.'

'Right,' I said. 'I thought you once said poetry was just your mum's big idea. What about the whole rock-chick thing you had going with Terry?'

'What? Oh that. That was just a thing. A phase thing. I know I'm really a born writer.' She hugged the poetry book to her chest. 'And we'll see if a certain gorgeous someone agrees with me.' She skipped away like a springtide lamb in love with new life. I watched her go and felt a familiar rock resting in my heart. I began to wonder how you live with a love that has no hope.

That lunch time, I made a private call from the school payphone. I spoke quickly and quietly to someone, then hung up. After school I skated on Orange Flyer to the bus stop. I jumped on board the public service to Ulverston, only I didn't travel all the way. I got off in the tiny village of Grizebeck, among hilly fields and high hedges. There was a pub set back from the main road called The Greyhound, and I waited outside it.

Only minutes later, a suited man wearing dark glasses came up to me. His hair was grey stubble on his scalp. He led me inside the pub, got me a lemonade and we sat down in a corner. He listened to everything I had to say, took a hand-drawn map from me, and made some notes. When I was through, he thanked me quietly and gave me my bus money. I refused his offer of a lift home, and hung around in the sunshine waiting for the next service back to Millom. But my heart was doing cartwheels, and I imagined sinister figures lurking in every wayside bush.

Even when I was safely aboard the bus, I sank low into my seat and went cold every time we stopped to pick someone up. Back in Millom, I skated home as fast as the Flyer would carry me. I sighed with relief to see our terraced house still standing.

That evening I wouldn't go further than my private garden. I needed the company of flowers, and the comfort of dark earth. Even though this BBC thing was on the radio, I'd take some samples of my work. I had a small patch of Lemon Circle daffodils, of Granddad's own breeding. Their petals were lacy white, with a trumpet lined in yellow like icing. It'd be good to show that not all daffs were a roaring golden colour.

I'd also take some of Granddad's notes, which were

stored on a shelf in the garage. Pages of his neatly sloping writing, with details of every floral experiment he ever tried. I could read them out, live on air, and maybe he'd be sitting close by to hear me, his hand resting warmly on my shoulder as I spoke of the great gifts he gave to this world.

Or my words might carry up to the morning clouds. And somewhere high over south Cumbria, in the sunless land, Granddad's heart would be young again with joy. But it wouldn't be a sunless place he'd gone to. Now there would always be sunlight there, because of the beautiful yellow flowers he must be planting and growing.

THIRTY-FOUR

The black-market price for gold is up to £400 per ounce. And so an amount the size of an ingot could fetch up to fifteen grand. These were the facts that went buzzing around Millom on the night of Malky's arrest. The cops also discovered gold turned into motorcycle parts, fitted onto his various bikes to smuggle out of the country.

The man I'd met in The Greyhound at Grizebeck was from the fraud squad. That's who I had phoned from school that day, after I realized where the gold ingots had to be. They sent him to get full details from me of where Terry's car sank. And because I'd spent so long staring at those tall grasses and bulrushes above the beach, I could pinpoint it exactly. There was an old road sign on the lane, right in line with where we'd crawled away.

The police even took my big idea on board. They arranged for a few dredgers to hit Morecambe Bay and churn up loads of sand. The council reported on the local news that it was to reduce the amount of sand on the beaches there. By doing this, they could be seen to find Terry's drowned car by accident. There was even a picture in the local paper of this giant earth mover, plucking out the buried car like it was a toy.

And who gave me that idea? None other than Malky himself, on the night we'd sat in darkness before Terry's motor got sucked under. It was Malky who'd gone on about the dredgers, and the quicksand build-up around the Duddon. He'd been trying to freak me out, but in the end it backfired on him.

It was those heavy clunks that Malky's rucksack had made. That was what I couldn't forget. The chunky weights inside it, and Terry's car sagging as Malky lobbed it into the back. No wonder he was in a foul mood later. Whoever he was meant to offload the ingots on in Manchester can't have turned up. No wonder he almost risked his life in the quicksand to get them back. And I'd thought it was only building bricks he was carrying.

All Malky's ingots were safely in the boot of Terry's car when the machine dug it up. I spent a few long nights waiting for our home to get smashed in. Malky might realize that one of us had worked out what his rucksack contained. But when the police took Malky away, and still nothing happened to me, I rested easier. And they finally towed his Porsche from our back alley, to confirm its owner's fingerprints on the ingots.

It was Malky who made me miss my granddad's last hours alive, so I thought it only right that I should help send him down for a few years. I wasn't called to give another statement or attend any trials. I just slipped back into the slumber of life in Millom, and tended my garden.

Sometimes I saw Diana Dowder in the streets,

hanging with the Bronx Crew. And she would give me a curious look, her freckly round face kind of suspicious. It was like she guessed something of my part in Malky's downfall, but never believed that such a simple sapling could pull it off. I think that's really what saved me. No one would believe, or dare to admit, that flower-loving Andrew Kindness had beaten the hard man. It wouldn't do much for Malky's image.

One night, when we passed on Dayton Street, I glanced back at Diana. She turned to face me, fluttered her eyelashes and slowly undid her trouser zip. Maybe she was trying to seduce me under Malky's orders, to get the truth. But I put my head down and hurried on. Once bitten by a Dowder, you should be very shy of getting mixed up again.

'Run off then, big baby!' she yelled after me. 'Go and snog yer soppy flowers.' And I did run – I ran so very fast. And what if I did kiss a daffodil later for comfort?

Soon enough it was the day of our Big Event in Hawkshead. Rehearsals at school had gone well, led by an inspired Angie. The morning was warm and blue, with clouds like sugar mountains over the estuary. By the time I skated to school, clutching bags of bulbs and books, there were three coaches waiting to carry us all.

Angie had saved a place for me beside her, near the front. Someone gave a loud wolf whistle from the back as I sat down. I pretended not to hear, and fiddled with the floral items I carried. Angie was jumpy, but probably because a certain windswept poet would soon be present. Mrs Hutchinson was coming along to give the whole thing a big write-up in her newspaper column. The Razzler had promised to get there too. Mum and Abayakurti would listen on the radio at work.

Angie nudged me and whispered, 'You OK? Nervous?'

I shook my head, though my guts were churning, and I went to the coach's toilet three times. I closed my eyes and tried to rehearse what I might say. *Breathe deeply,* Mum had said. *Speak slowly. Breathe from your centre, and imagine a warm light inside your heart.* Which is easier said than done with half the nation tuned in.

The coaches rolled along towards Coniston, with a great lake sparkling through the trees on our right. Flat green meadows were alive with frisky lambs. Our vehicle was the last in line, and the driver hit his brakes suddenly. He'd spotted one of the lambs with its daft little head stuck in a wire fence. We all piled off the bus as the driver wrestled with tight squares of steel meshing. We cheered him on, but the other sheep just grazed away as if in dreamland. The lamb kicked up a right bleating fuss, and toddled off without a glance of thanks when it was free.

Then it was uphill through shady pine forests, where the sun's rays never filter. And finally into Hawkshead, a village so cosy and tidy that some people call it 'Toy Town'. They sell Beatrix Potter by the jackpot there, and many other sweet nothings that foreign tourists might buy.

The old grammar school where Wordsworth went is made of white rough cast. It's the kind of pebbledash coating you get on many Cumbrian houses and buildings. A mounted sundial sticks out over the front door like a fallen star. The window and door frames are all done with red sandstone.

A white van stood on the gravel, with BBC OUTSIDE BROADCAST along the side. Various techies with wires and headsets were bumbling about. We all piled off the coaches and were led into the schoolroom downstairs. The place is a preserved museum piece now, but you get a taste of what it was like back then. A pulley device hangs down from the rafters and the beams above. Legend has it that boys were strapped in there to be whipped with a birch.

The ancient desks, blackened with age, were all shoved to the sides. One of them is said to have Wordsworth's name carved on it, done by William himself, and we all buzzed around trying to find it. The teacher's own larger desk stood near the front. You could imagine poor kids and orphans in grubby skirts and shorts being bawled at by some stern ogre. The chatter of lost children still echoed.

Wordsworth first went there when he was nine. The headmaster was called the Reverend Taylor, and he used to lend the young William his own poetry books. By the time he was seventeen, Wordsworth was heading south to college in Cambridge.

Someone tapped me on the back and took me outside to do a sound test. I babbled my name and address into a furry mic. By now I could feel a sense of panic setting in.

'Take your time,' said this blond guy, hardly older than me. 'Speak slowly and clearly, and don't rush. OK?'

I swallowed hard and nodded. Another tap on my back. It was Angie with the handsome poet. My heart sank to a new low. He ran a hand through his manly head of dark hair. Angie introduced him and he smiled. He said, 'I'm really looking forward to your little talk.'

I smiled back through my sulks. 'Thanks,' I said. 'I wish *I* was.'

Almost before I knew it, we were lined up in that chilly old schoolroom. I was right at the front, opposite Angie, who looked flushed and anxious. Then some speccy boffin from the BBC came forward, said his name and told us to remain silent through the intro. At a signal from outside, he began, mic in hand.

'William Wordsworth's famous poem about daffodils was written two centuries ago. It was a couple of years since he'd seen the flowers that inspired his verses, when walking by Ullswater on a stormy day with his sister Dorothy . . .'

We all fidgeted and choked back coughs. Angie fixed everyone with a strict eye.

'. . . Two hundred years on from the first-known

version of "Daffodils", we are gathered at Wordsworth's old grammar school in Hawkshead. I am joined by a hundred pupils from nearby Millom Comprehensive. Among them is lower sixth former Angela Hutchinson, already an award-winning poet herself. And she will now lead her fellow students through a reading of Wordsworth's celebrated ode to daffodils.'

Angie stepped forward, her face red, her hair aflame. She raised a hand and breathed in. We all sucked air into our lungs too. On Angie's count of three we began.

THIRTY-FIVE

Our voices came booming out with such force that the show's presenter stepped back. He made a calming motion with both hands. We toned it down a bit, but everyone was high on adrenalin and the Big Moment. Angie stood chopping the air like a conductor, trying to keep us all in time together.

> '. . . Beside the lake . . . beneath the trees,
> Fluttering and dancing . . . in the breeze.'

And that was the first verse finished with. So far, so good. But then my stupid brain went blank. I'd stared at the words so many times to get them perfect, and now the whole lot had vanished. I gave thanks that everyone else was coping with the occasion, and joined back in as my memory restored itself. And yet very soon my emotions were running riot again. And it was these few lines that did me in.

> 'Continuous . . . as the stars that shine
> And twinkle on the Milky Way,
> They stretched . . . in never-ending line
> Along the margin of a bay.'

All I could imagine was my granddad, safe among the stars somewhere, and listening proudly. I pictured him planting that tree of life with Golden Glories for those two vanished tourists. I remembered the long hours in his back garden, learning the sweet secrets of a daffodil's heart. His gentle voice, rich with northern poetry, quoting the names of his precious cross-breeding creations.

'Dutch Beauty . . . Isle of Arran . . . Cello Strings . . . Angel Wings . . . Walking Boots . . . Girl Friend . . .'

I felt his presence so strongly. And with Angie swaying before me, and the choral throng of voices all around, I caved in. Fat sploshy tears ran down my pudding cheeks. I tried to swipe them away, but more followed in a flood. I gave a loud hiccup, which I thought must echo into every living room worldwide. Angie stared at me in alarm. Even that didn't control my great blubbing. I hiccupped again.

> 'I gazed and gazed . . . but little thought
> What wealth the show to me had brought.'

We were heading into the last verse now. Someone nudged me sharply from the side. I sniffed loudly, my throat all clogged up. Everything was a bright blur of wetness. Angie was still gawping, as if I'd taken down my trousers. I could just make out the BBC presenter gazing at me too, with wide eyes. I could hear him thinking, *Isn't he the one we've got lined up for interview in a minute? Heaven help us.*

Somehow I pulled myself together for the final stanza. The door to the schoolroom was open, and I saw my dad's punky head poking in. Mrs Hutchinson was right behind him, trying to see over his big shoulders. Some guy from the local press was lurking there with a camera. I swiped a sleeve across my eyes and took a deep breath.

> *'For oft when on my couch I lie*
> *In vacant or in pensive mood . . .'*

Angie was all beaming smiles now, with the end in sight. Our voices rose again, as if to signal a job well done. Some guy in that BBC trailer outside was probably doing his nut trying to control the sound levels.

> *'They flash upon that inward eye*
> *Which is the bliss . . . of solitude . . .'*

My throat still had a big lump that I couldn't swallow. And I knew the last two lines might crack me up again, so I whispered them below the big noise made by everyone else. For the closing couplet, Angie slowed us all right down.

> *'And then . . . my heart . . with pleasure fills,*
> *And dances . . . with . . . the daffodils.'*

Angie sliced the air to hush everyone. The old school-room went deathly quiet. Then came one last loud hiccup in the sudden silence. That was me. I squeezed my eyes and blushed. People were starting to giggle, which was the cue for that presenter bloke to step forward and blether again.

'Thank you very much, pupils from Millom Comprehensive, led by Angela Hutchinson. In a few moments we will be talking to one of the students here. A young man who has some intriguing secrets to share with us, all about the cross-breeding of daffodils. But first, a word with Dennis Turner, who is the curator of Wordsworth's old grammar school, here in Hawkshead . . .'

Angie rushed forward and held my arms. 'Are you OK?' she cried. 'Come here, let's get you sorted out.' Grabbing my hand, she took me upstairs to a little wash-room. She splashed water on my red face, and dried it with paper towels.

'OK, just take it easy,' she said. 'You'll be fine. You know your stuff so well. Just keep it simple, and remember that the listeners can't see what you're talking about, so describe it for them. That's all you have to do. Right?'

'Right,' I said. I went all woozy. 'No, it's not all right. Help me, my stomach's turning.' I turned towards the sink, my guts heaving.

And that's when it happened. The most marvellous moment of my life. A few seconds of such sudden bliss that I felt reborn. All I knew was Angie holding my head in her two lovely hands. She lowered her face towards me. I felt the soft press of her moist lips on mine. My eyes closed, as if to hold this fleeting dream for ever. Then came a slight pop as our mouths parted. But I was many miles away, being dipped in a blue river, with my whole life washed clean. There was no fear any more.

'Now then,' said Angie softly. 'Nothing to be scared of.'

I swayed like a sleepwalker, slowly shaking my head to agree. Someone called out our names from downstairs. It sounded urgent.

'Time to go,' said Angie. 'The rest of your life begins right now.'

The next thing I recall, we were outside in bright sunshine. All my papers and flowers were laid on an old desk. A big BBC mic was thrust at me. I was introduced to the world, and asked a question I hardly heard. It didn't matter though, because I was soon nattering away like an old pro.

Angie was right – this was the moment I was born to. I felt her admiring gaze like a warm lantern at my back.

'All daffodils are made up of what's called the perianth,' I said, 'which is basically their ring of bright petals, and the inner trumpet, which holds the stigma. The tiny specks of pollen are what you transfer from one species to another, in order to cross-breed them. So what you need is a Seed Bearer, and a Pollen Parent . . .'

The presenter kept nodding at me like he'd got some

awkward tic. His cheesy smiles were meant to be calming, but felt weird. I was aware of The Razzler to one side, drinking what looked like bottled pond weed. I talked away as if I was alone in my little garden. I went on about anthers and ovules and seed pods. All the time I could feel the gentle crush of Angie's lips. My heart was leaping higher than heaven.

The BBC guy interrupted me. 'I believe, Andrew, that you learned this unusual talent from your granddad. Was there any special occasion that inspired you to follow in his footsteps? Any incident that made you realize this was your calling?'

I stared into his expensive designer specs. For a moment I was back on the estuary, six years ago. The presenter frowned at my silence. In his glinting glasses I saw two doomed figures in the quicksand, then my granddad's tree-shaped Golden Glories.

I began to stammer for the first time. This part wasn't in my planned script.

'N-nothing special,' I said. 'N-not that I recall. But I think that ... flowers like these c-can spread lots of happiness. Most of all to people who've suffered in some way. Maybe that's to do with all their bright colours. It's a bit like bringing, um, sunshine to the sunless. Yeah? I think that's in a Wordsworth poem too.'

The speccy boffin looked relieved. 'Indeed it is!' he gushed. 'And what a very fitting way to bring this morning's programme to an end. Thank you to all the staff and pupils from Millom who helped arrange the reading, to the curator of . . .'

And that was it. My five minutes of fame under the Cumbrian sun. Angie rushed over to hug me, the handsome poet patted my back, and The Razzler was busy chatting up my English teacher.

A lunch buffet was laid on for us in the old schoolroom, but we all sat outside eating and buzzing. Even some of the drongos who had ruined that first rehearsal seemed chuffed. They swaggered about like stars on a movie set. I smiled at them.

Me and Angie had pulled it off together. I sat on a low wall with a plate of sarnies, watching Angie blush and gush with her poet. And I knew we would never be together like I dreamed. I could never be what she wanted. I would always be simple Andrew Kindness, alone with his flowers, and Angie would be a girl everyone would notice. Her talents would take her higher than I could ever fly.

But she wouldn't forget me now, not ever. Not after today. I would always be there, in a tiny corner of her heart. And years from now, or whenever she saw daffodils, I would rise up and remind her of one spring morning in Hawkshead.

Maybe it's enough to be loved in that way.

THIRTY-SIX

On the Saturday morning after our triumph, Dad found me in my garden. He was still following his Gerson regime, with Mum's help, although we were both sworn to secrecy about the reasons for it. Dad's mates thought he was just on a long overdue detox.

'Hope you're not busy,' he said. 'You've got a full day ahead.'

I dropped the trowel I was holding. My giant corkscrew scutcher lay on the turned earth beside me. 'A full day of what?' I asked.

Dad grinned and tapped his nose. 'Get yourself scrubbed up,' he said. 'Then meet me back here in ten minutes. I've put some clean clothes on your bed.'

I sighed and shrugged, then went indoors to follow orders. Shortly after, when I was fresh and tidy, I went out the back again. And there was The Razzler in his open-top sports car, with Angie sitting in the front beside him. She waved shyly.

'Huh?' I said. 'What gives?'

Dad pushed open the side door. 'Just get in, your lord-ship,' he said. 'And see what the sweet morning brings.'

It was almost midday, and the sun sat in its high

heaven. This was easily the year's hottest day so far. We drove uphill out of Millom towards Broughton, where I guessed we might be heading for a pub lunch. The bay was blue and golden behind us, and all around were fresh green fields of sheep. Only we didn't go on to Broughton, but pulled off the main road near the Duddon bridge. Dad got out and grabbed a picnic hamper from the boot, which he gave to Angie. She whispered something to him and he nodded. He tapped his watch, then got back into his red motor. 'See ya later,' he said, and roared off with a dusty spurt.

My poor heart was twisting and rolling again, with Angie so close by. Was she going to torture me for ever?

But she said, 'This is your reward for helping me out. I reckon we had a big success. You see the *Evening Mail*'s front page about us?'

Of course I had. And so far no one had laughed at my strange hobby, or offered to punch my pathetic lights out. I nodded, and hung my head low. There was only one reward I really wanted from Angie, being honest, and it involved the sweet smudge of her lips on mine again.

She seemed to read my mind, and patted my hair. 'Let's have a walk,' she said. 'Then your dad's made us some nice grub.'

The river Duddon wasn't very wide at this point. Just an easy stone's throw across. But it was crystal clear, cool and calming. We wandered slowly along its green verge together, stopping to take in the endless details on display.

The sandy banks were drilled with holes where some insects or other had burrowed in to breed. Scaly bark lay on the slender riverside trees. Catkins fell from their branches into the water, to float like caterpillars.

'Wow,' said Angie. 'You can really smell the freshness of wild water.'

We saw the iron red of the river bed's rocks. Once there were furnaces sited right along the Duddon. Now there's just remains and reminders of the great iron industry.

Tiny fish were turning and darting, the colour of mud-brown stones. Wild blossom trees sent their white petals floating downstream. 'It looks like confetti,' said Angie. 'Wouldn't it be fun getting married in a river? You'd have to be half naked.'

We walked from the stony bridge, up the steep gorge along a narrow road. Across the way stood a rising upland of trees. They wore every colour of springtime, before summer could turn them all the same shade. Pitch-dark emerald, lime green, forest green. And those trees that were just budding left a misty pink haze.

Two silver birches stood together, the same age and height. One was in full leaf, the other hardly in flower. One living and one dying, side by side. On another far hillside lay a scorched patch of dead pines. They were no more than standing stumps. Something unseen, unknown, in the climate had killed them. Dark invisible forces at work.

A single buzzard came circling in the blue sky. We watched it flapping like a scrap of old leather. At last it dropped like an arrow for the killing.

And then, just like old Willy Wordsworth, we stumbled on a patch of daffodils. The last of the season's finest, now browning like old paper. I showed Angie the sexy bits inside one of the flowers.

'These smaller stems are the anthers, OK? They hold the pollen for when bees and things go sniffing inside. The bees brush this pollen onto the stigma, which is that bigger stalk in the middle. Then the pollen works its way down to fertilize the seeds. When the flower dies, the yellow head part shrivels away. The seed pod just below it swells up, then bursts and scatters the seeds.'

Angie rubbed her slender white neck. 'Wow,' she said. 'Sweet. I'm getting all hot and bothered just thinking about it.'

She wasn't the only one. Angie's warm breath, mixed with spring sunshine and daffodil perfumes, was enough to melt me. I gave her a yearning look, like a helpless seal. She ignored it with a quick smile and stood up. 'Let's go eat,' she said, checking her watch. 'It's after one o'clock.'

So we sat by the Duddon again, with our healthy lunch. I think Mum had been involved too as there was home-made pizza, avocado dip, asparagus and fennel salad, veggie samosas and a bottle of fresh fruit smoothie. We sat and sunbathed, and ate almost everything. Then we talked about that morning in Hawkshead, laughing at my sorry hiccups and taking the mickey out of Angie's own weird poetry.

She checked her watch so often that I got annoyed. 'You got another date?' I asked.

'Sort of,' she said. 'And so have you. Ah, right, here's your dad back.' She quickly gathered up the picnic remains and stuffed them in the basket.

'Where now?' I asked.

'You'll see,' said Angie. 'Come along.'

Dad sat with his engine purring. 'Lunch OK?' he asked.

'Brill,' said Angie. 'Nothing left, I'm afraid. Drive on, driver.'

Dad revved away and took the road through Broughton and down into Foxfield. I still thought we were just popping out for a drink, maybe to the Prince of Wales in Foxfield, where Dad loved the home-brewed beer. He'd not had a drink since I couldn't remember when. He was bound to crack soon, especially as the test results on his cancer were quite promising. It seemed like he'd found the danger in time, and a simple operation would be enough.

But we passed through Foxfield, and slowly made our way down to Kirkby-in-Furness. From there it was a clear view across the estuary back to Millom. We pulled up near the sleepy little railway station, with its iron bridge spanning the tracks. A small boy was up on the bridge, waiting for local sprinter trains to wave at.

Dad parked by the station, and I followed him and Angie over the bridge. We came out on dry marshland and found a group of other people there. Many wore sun-hats and loose clothing, or carried field glasses and maps. We joined up with them.

'What gives?' I asked Angie. 'Who are these lot?'

A goods train rolled through Kirkby station with end-less wagons in tow. That boy on the bridge was smiling happily as the great weight thundered below him.

Angie took my hand gently. 'We're going to walk across the sands together,' she said. 'You and me. It's time you buried this fear of them. I mean, you managed to save us both on Morecambe Bay that night. And that was quicksand we crawled over. You'll never leave the past behind unless you face up to what happened six years ago.'

I backed off. 'No way,' I said. 'Haven't you realized? I'm bad news where any sand is concerned. There's bound to be a disaster if I go along.'

Angie smiled. 'Look,' she said, 'it's a guided walking tour. An official tour party that goes out every day. They know the tides like you know your daffodils.'

I felt my heart jumping. I shook my head.

Angie held out her fingers. 'What if I hold your hand very tightly?' she said. 'All the way across.'

This was outrageous blackmail, and she knew it. 'You mean, *all* the way?' I asked.

Angie nodded. She really meant it.

Heck . . . an hour of holding the most precious palm on earth! I'd have swum through Morecambe Bay at midnight for the chance.

Angie said, 'I won't leave you.'

'Promise?' I whispered.

'Promise.'

The tour party was getting ready to move off. I looked back at Dad, who waved and smiled. 'I've got Orange Flyer in the car,' he said, 'if you really want it.'

I gripped Angie's warm palm. 'It's OK,' I said. 'I'll manage without.'

And then we were away, over the grassy marshes where huge lumps had been eroded like jigsaw pieces. Then came the sands themselves, but they seemed like an eternal desert to cross. And that's when I first weakened. I hung back, but felt Angie tug me forward like a dog on its lead. Her smile was all sunny, her cheekbones lifting with joy up to those blue eyes.

I closed my eyes, being led along like a blind boy. I made small talk to silence the scary screams in my mind.

'Did you know,' I said, 'that only about one per cent of our genes really defines us as human? We actually share a third of our genes with daffodils. Which means our DNA makes us thirty-three and a third per cent daffodil. That's neat, yeah?'

I felt Angie stop right beside me. Her soft fingers prised open my eyes. 'I never knew that,' she said. 'You should have mentioned it during that BBC programme.'

I was being pulled forward again. 'Yeah,' I agreed. 'I wish I had now. And did you know that daffodils—?'

Angie laughed, and almost doubled up. 'Sssh!' she said. 'Talk about something else for once. How you ever gonna get a girlfriend with a one-track mind?'

I didn't know the answer to that. There was only one girl I had ever wanted, and here she was being my guardian angel across the landscape of my nightmares. And then I needed a pee because my insides were tight with dread. My bladder was prickling, but not for the world would I have had a leak near Angie.

I looked around and got my bearings. The route we were taking would pass close to the site of that accident I'd witnessed. I let myself be dragged along, scraping as close to Angie as I dared without getting too cosy. I kept my eyes on the burning beach below me, quite certain that everything would soon dissolve into sludge.

But the golden ground stayed firm. Seabirds glided on the soft breeze above, and the shoreline beckoned from what felt like miles ahead. The sands began to get more churned up, and turned into wider furrows. It was hard to keep your footing in places. Before I knew it we were halfway across, and heading for the site of that tragedy. I couldn't say exactly where it was, but I had seen it so often in my mind's eye.

Putting my free hand in my jeans pocket, I felt some small and grainy bits. They were daffodil seeds, and tiny bulbs, left over from one of my recent plantings.

As the tour guide nattered on and pointed out the names of the looming mountains, I stopped. Angie got tugged back by me, but I wouldn't let go of her hand. Using my free one, I knelt down to scoop a hole in the sand. And in went those few daffodil seeds, and one small bulb, although they would never flourish in a place where the tides washed over. But I had tried once more to make my peace with two strangers who I could never really have helped. I hoped they were watching me, and knew how heavy my guilt had been.

'Will those grow out here?' asked Angie.

'No,' I said. 'But I've nothing else to offer. It's all I can ever seem to give.'

'It's more than most people do,' said Angie, and I knew she was right.

We chased after the other walkers, just in case my worst nightmares opened up suddenly and we were left stranded. And there among the group of thirty was Mrs Tyson. My old junior school teacher, whose husband's grave I had decorated with a heart of Mystic daffs.

She carried a small rucksack like the one that had leaked my pee many years back. 'Hello, Andrew.' She smiled. 'And Angela. What a wonderful broadcast you gave on the radio. Andrew, I had no idea you were so attached to daffodils. You must call by the churchyard one day. My husband is buried there, and the most amazing crop of daffodils burst out by his resting place this year. Maybe you can explain how flowers arrange themselves in such patterns. You might know what variety they are too. Do call on me one day, and we can go down there together.'

She went off to walk with someone else. The bay was blue and brown all about us. Millom and its coastline were in view now. You could see the old iron jetty, and the crumbled wooden posts where great ships once pulled up. A few sailboats were beached near the shore.

'What was Mrs Tyson on about?' asked Angie.

Part of me wanted to explain. Maybe Angie would think I was all lovely and generous if I told her. But it wouldn't change anything between us. She would never yearn to hold me, or to keep me, even if I planted a million hearts of Mystics.

'Not really sure,' I replied. 'But she did me a big favour one time. I'll tell you about it, but promise not to laugh.'

'I promise.'

'And you'll never tell anyone else?'

'Promise that too.'

We were in sight of The Slaggy now, baking with its whiteness under the sun. 'OK,' I said. 'Well, there was this junior school trip about six years ago, right. And we went off to Dove Cottage, only I drank too much water and orange juice . . .'

THIRTY-SEVEN

We made it safely ashore, of course. Then everyone went their separate ways, except for me and Angie. It was like we both wanted to spin the day out a bit longer.

We headed for a local landmark called The Plug. It's another relic from the days when iron ore was mined here. The ore got shoved into a giant closed furnace, with the heat cranked up. This removed the metal elements, which became liquid when melted. And like my granddad often said, the impure scum was skimmed by a bar and dumped to one side. It sat under the main furnace to go cold, then got shovelled out.

But the very last load ever mined here was dropped while it was still hot. And when it finally cooled, it left an almost volcanic deposit of dark mineral.

I stroked the huge and blackened sphere in memory of my granddad. Maybe he'd even watched as this final lot of iron-ore debris was dumped from the furnace.

Nearby was a shallow and soggy pool, all wet and wild on the scrubland. We saw a little Natterjack toad basking in the sun, its skin a mosaic of light and dark brown. It stared dumbly at us with black eyes. Its bulging throat swelled up like a balloon of glass, blown through a glass blower's tube, ready for the furnace. Then it deflated like bubble gum around a child's mouth.

We took the rough coastal road around the bay, where my granddad used to find iron nuggets and tell me they were gold ingots. The wind whipped in and almost blew us sideways. Me and Angie held onto each other, laughing at the sudden gusts. We stood with our backs to the big lighthouse, trying to take shelter from the gale. I held the hem of Angie's coat as her red-blonde hair was blown against my face. And I slipped a few tiny daffodil seeds into her pocket.

We went into the observation hut to recover, looking out over the blue lagoons. Dark blue waves rippled under the sea wind. Millom's little inland ocean looked stormy that day. A flat island in the middle was crowded with wild birds.

The old sea wall is broken halfway across the first lagoon, and there's a little step leading down from it. Two kids in swimming trunks were getting ready to swim. They didn't seem to care about the windy weather, as the sunlight was so summery. I watched them dive in, and then surface with laughing gasps. Way below them, the old mining works rotted slowly away.

On a wall chart inside the long hut, people had listed all the different birds they'd seen there recently. Sand martins, willow warblers, moorhens, lapwings, sparrowhawks, kestrels, curlews, cormorants, grey herons, Canada geese. Both birds and bird-watchers flock to the lagoons as they offer such a peaceful sanctuary.

In the distance, beyond Millom, the powdery blue mountains were jostling together. They stood shoulder to craggy shoulder, like runners waiting to race.

Then me and Angie went out and rested on The Blocks for a while. Those great concrete cubes were warm under the sun. The sea crashed in and broke up into lazy spirals below.

Each of The Blocks lay at an angle, like playing cards ready to collapse. We sat back to back, with our spines against a sharp ridge. Flossy clouds above wore a steely shade below, hinting at the rain to come. The sea wind was cold in my eyes, and loosened a few tears. Angie smiled and smoothed them away. She thought I was crying at all the beauty and sadness of the day. But I wasn't crying, honestly, although I might have done in private later. I tied up the loose lace on one of Angie's walking boots. She tilted her face to the blustery sun, and smiled with closed eyes.

It was the last time we were ever really alone together.

It's strange how the tourist board never seem to bring their cameras to Millom. OK, so we don't have the teashops of Keswick, or the great lake at Windermere. And our strange little streets aren't lined with old cobbles or thatched pubs. But there's so much wild beauty here that people never see, and so much tough history. And I think it's a shame to bury the town away like a poor relation.

If you come here in spring when the daffs are out, or when bee orchids are blooming near The Slaggy, you'll know what I mean. Take a windblown wander along the beaches, and stand near The Plug to remember times past. And you can picture the roaring inferno of the blast furnaces. The giant towers, draped in metal to protect them from German bombers. The steam trains pulling wagons of iron ore to the foundry.

I imagine another train, with a great bucket at the front, tipping the iron slag into the sea. The red-hot remains making a great white flare as they shoot up and sizzle. And my Granddad Hebthwaite, learning to skim off the scum and find precious nuggets below. It's all here still, in the earth and in the memory. And now you know how to find us. We'll be waiting.

As for The Razzler, it turned out he'd found his 'little lump' in good time. They managed to operate, and keep all his manly tackle intact. But the scare it gave him never quite left, and he didn't go back to his mad old ways. My mum kept in closer contact with Dad, and his Gerson therapy of pure health seemed to restore him.

He went back to his window cleaning, and had to modernize with the times. But with Malky inside for a while, there were fewer broken windows to mend locally. And so my dad set up a more serious sideline in car repairs, which meant he had to declare all the cash he used to pocket in private. And some of his taste in loud music was sweetened by the presence of classical concertos to meditate with. Long piano solos replaced some of the endless guitar workouts in his collection.

Mum didn't go off to Skyros that summer. She put family matters first, but believed she might one day make a new life out there. And good old Abayakurti stayed around, offering his blessings and kind smiles to all. He never faced me about sexual herbs again, and anyway it was a while before I'd got such things on the brain. The offers that came my way after the BBC broadcast were endless. I spent half that summer in garden centres and such like, boring people's pants off about rare daffodils.

After one of those events, a lady in her thirties whispered in my ear, and offered to show me 'the ways of the world'. She was a tomato grower from Kendal, with scary pink lipstick on her teeth. I told her you shouldn't cross-breed daffodil types with vegetable types. I think I had a narrow escape . . .

Angie remained on the straight and narrow into the upper sixth form. I scraped through enough exams to stay on the following year, when at least I saw more of her. She kept on winning all these prizes, and her mum kept nagging my dad for news of his Motor Heads group. As for them, they finally got their own car built from scratch. It looked pretty good too, until one of the Bronx Crew nicked it one night and smashed the front in. But at least that gave the group an excuse to keep going, and repair it.

We learned that Malky finished up in Haverigg prison, just around the coast. His mansion was under police observation for some time. I knew he'd be out again soon enough, and maybe he'd come looking for me with a few hard questions. I sometimes thought of Malky, and his quest for a piece of perfect gold. And there was me, with my own quest for perfect golden creations in nature. It made me smile.

So what if Malky tried to find me? I'd got plans to be away by then. There was a university in Cumbria, with several campuses, where you could study gardening and other natural stuff. I'd be OK out in the big wide world, especially as I'd suddenly grown taller. My special Orange Flyer skateboard got hidden away in the cupboard, along with all those old iron nuggets. And as my ears slowly took on a more normal shape, I also stashed Mum's woolly hat there too.

Granddad's grave grew an extra April Tears daffodil every spring. Soon there was a large patch of them, blooming over his heart. And I planted a single 'Angie' flower among them too, scooping the earth out with my scutcher.

I kept a close eye on Granddad's tree-shape of Golden Glories beside the bay. It's funny how it was always left alone, even though graffiti got sprayed everywhere and wooden benches around the bay were ripped apart. Maybe some things are so precious that the destroyers can't even see them there.

And on warm spring evenings, I still like to stand on The Blocks and look out over the bay. As the sunset strokes me with gold, I remember what I once witnessed out there. I wait until the moon emerges, turning the waves to a ghostly green. And I try to give thanks for whatever my own life has brought me so far.

Granddad once told me that to truly love this life, you need to know its darkest corners. But if you can bring a bit of sunshine to the sunless, it can only be for the good. I mean, what else are we really here for on this earth? Think about it some day, when the spring mornings look so golden and green.